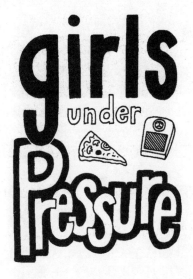

Also available by Jacqueline Wilson and
published by Doubleday/Corgi
GIRLS IN LOVE

And for younger readers, published by
Corgi Yearling
THE LOTTIE PROJECT
BAD GIRLS
THE BED AND BREAKFAST STAR
DOUBLE ACT
THE MUM-MINDER
THE STORY OF TRACY BEAKER
THE SUITCASE KID
CLIFFHANGER
BURIED ALIVE!
GLUBBSLYME

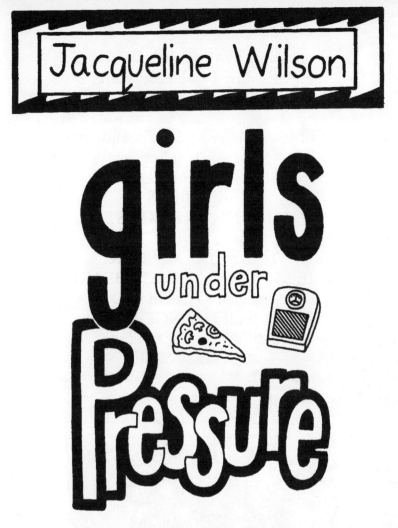

Jacqueline Wilson

# girls under Pressure

**Illustrated by Nick Sharratt**

## DOUBLEDAY
LONDON · NEW YORK · TORONTO · SYDNEY · AUCKLAND

TRANSWORLD PUBLISHERS LTD
61–63 Uxbridge Road, London, W5 5SA

TRANSWORLD PUBLISHERS (AUSTRALIA) PTY LTD
15–25 Helles Avenue, Moorebank, NSW 2170

TRANSWORLD PUBLISHERS (NZ) LTD
3 William Pickering Drive, Albany, Auckland

DOUBLEDAY CANADA LTD
105 Bond Street, Toronto, Ontario M5B 1Y3

Published in 1998 by Doubleday
a division of Transworld Publishers Ltd

A catalogue record for this book is available
from the British Library

ISBN 0 385 408056

Set in 13/16pt Bembo by
Phoenix Typesetting, Ilkley, West Yorkshire

Made and printed in Great Britain by
Mackays of Chatham PLC, Chatham, Kent

For Theano Petrou

# Chapter One

# Modelgirl

It's all my idea.

'Let's go Christmas shopping on Saturday,' I say to my two best friends, Magda and Nadine.

'Great,' says Magda, who lives to shop.

'Sure,' says Nadine, but she looks surprised. 'I thought you always made your own Christmas presents, Ellie.'

'Yes, well, I think I've grown out of that stage now,' I say hurriedly.

We've always had this silly tradition in my family. I'd think of a theme and then make everyone a present based on it. There was the year of the stripy hand-knitted scarves, the wobbly vases the year I joined the pottery class, the cross-stitched canvas purses . . . I made them for everyone, friends as well as family, and because people were polite I thought they really *liked* my loopy home-made junk.

I've known Nadine since we were both five so she's endured years of fraying dresses for her Barbie dolls and lumpy little felt mice. When we started secondary school I made Nadine a black and silver friendship bracelet. I made one for Magda in pink and purple. They seemed to like them. They both wore them for a while anyway.

Last Christmas I made special boxes for all the family, studded with beads and shells. I used liquorice allsorts for Eggs's box – but he tried to lick them through the glaze and hurt his tongue. Typical. Dad and Anna act like he's an infant prodigy but *I* think he's got the brains of a flea. I pondered long and hard over boxes for Magda and Nadine. In the end I made Nadine a silver box with a painted silver shell design. I did an identical one in gold for Magda. She opened hers as if she was expecting something inside – and then she asked if I'd be making her a gold necklace to go in it next year. She was joking – I *think*. I suddenly felt about Eggs's age.

'We'll go round the Flowerfields Shopping Centre,' I say firmly. 'We'll buy all the presents for our families, and then we'll split up for a bit and buy each other stuff.'

'And then we'll go to the Soda Fountain and have a milkshake,' says Magda, getting more enthusiastic by the minute.

The Soda Fountain recently opened up on the Flowerfields basement floor. It's like those shiny ice cream parlour places you see in old American movies.

It's become the in place to hang out now – rumoured to be great for meeting boys. If there's one thing Magda likes better than shopping, it's boys. Lots of them.

Nadine sighs and raises her eyebrows at me. She's seriously off the opposite sex at the moment, ever since she got heavily involved with this creep Liam who was just using her. She doesn't want to go out with anyone else now. Magda wants to go out with a different boy every night. I'm not sure what I want. And it's not like I get that many offers anyway.

Well. There's this boy Dan I met on holiday. He's my *sort-of* boyfriend. I don't see him much because he lives in Manchester. And he's younger than me. And looks a bit weird. He is definitely not a dream-boat.

I shall have to get him a Christmas present though. Goodness knows what. I've had this sudden brilliant idea of buying Magda and Nadine underwear from Knickerbox. Red satin flowery knickers for Magda. Black lace for Nadine. And then I could get Dad a big pair of Marks and Sparks boxer shorts and Anna some pretty prim white panties. Eggs could have Mickey Mouse knickers. I've been warming to the universal knicker present. But I can't give Dan *underpants*! Though I know exactly what sort, a wacky pair with a silly message . . .

I decide I'll have a good look round on Saturday and see if I get any further inspiration. I go over to Nadine's house around ten. Her dad's outside, washing his car. He's the sort of guy who worships his car, spending hours and hours annointing it every weekend.

'Hello, Curlynob,' he calls.

I force a cheery grin and knock at the door. Nadine's mum answers, in an old jumper and leggings, with a J-cloth in her hand. She is obviously dressed for serious house-cleaning.

'Hello, dear. Nadine's in her bedroom,' she says, sniffing disapprovingly.

'Hello, Ellie. I'm helping Mummy,' says Natasha, waving a feather duster from the living room.

Natasha is still in her cutsie-pie pyjamas and fluffy slippers. She's dancing round to some silly cartoon music on the telly, flicking her feather duster as she goes.

'Isn't she a good girl?' says Nadine's mum proudly.

I try to manufacture another smile.

Natasha rushes at me.

'You look dirty, Ellie,' she says. She prances round me, poking her feathers right in my face. 'There! I'm wiping all the dust off.'

'Oh, *sweet*!' says her mum.

'Ouch! Natasha, that *hurts*,' I say, my smile now very sickly indeed.

Natasha is the only six year old in the world *worse* than my little brother Eggs. I sidle past and run up the stairs to Nadine's room. It is wonderfully black and bleak after the glaring patterns in the hall. Nadine is looking glamourously black and bleak herself, her long black hair hanging loose, her eyes heavily outlined with black kohl, her face powdered white as chalk. She's wearing a black skimpy sweater, black jeans, black boots – and as I come into her room she pulls on her black velvet jacket.

'Hi. What are those weird red marks on your face, Ellie?'

'Your delightful sister has just been seriously assaulting me with her feather duster.'

'Oh, God. Sorry. Don't worry. She wants a new Barbie doll for Christmas. I'll customize one. How about Killer Barbie, with a special sharp little dagger that whips out of her dinky stiletto?'

'Remember all our Barbie doll games, Naddie? I liked it when we turned them all into witches best.'

'Oh yeah, you made them all those little black frocks and special hooked noses out of plasticine. Wicked.'

We both sigh nostalgically.

'I used to *love* playing with plasticine,' I say. 'I still like mucking around with Eggs's little set, though he's got all the colours mixed up.'

'OK, then. That's your Christmas present solved. Your very own pack of plasticine,' says Nadine. 'I don't know what I'm going to get Magda though. She was hinting like mad about this new Chanel nail varnish but I bet it costs a fortune.'

'I know. I'm a bit strapped for cash too, actually.'

'It's all right for Magda. Her mum and dad give her that socking great allowance. My dad gives me exactly the same as Natasha, for God's sake. In fact Natasha ends up with heaps more because they're forever buying her extra stuff. It's so lousy having a sucky little sister.'

'Just as bad with a boring little brother. That's why Magda's so lucky, because *she's* the spoilt baby of the family.'

Magda certainly shows stylish evidence of spoiling when we meet up with her at the Flowerfields Shopping Centre entrance. She's wearing a brand new bright red furry jacket that looks wonderful.

'Is that your Christmas present, Magda?' Nadine asks.

'Of course not! No, I had a little moan to Mum that although my leather jacket is ultra hip it isn't really *warm* – so she had a word with Dad and we went on a little shopping trip and *voilà!*' She twirls round in the jacket, turning up the collar and striking poses like a fashion model.

'It looks fantastic, Magda,' I say enviously. 'Hey, what about your leather jacket then? Don't you want it any more?'

I've been longing for a leather jacket like Magda's for *months*. I've tried dropping hints at home. Hints! I've made brazen pleas. To no avail. Dad and Anna won't listen. I have to put up with my boring boring boring old coat that doesn't do a thing for me. It makes me look dumpier than ever. I *know* it's too tight over my bum. I'd have sold my soul for Magda's soft supple stylish leather – but now her furry scarlet jacket is even *better*.

Nadine fiddles at Magda's neck to have a deck at the label.

'Wow! *Whistles*,' says Nadine.

She bought her black velvet at Camden Market. It's a bit shabby and stained now, but it still looks good on her. Anything looks good on Nadine because she's so tall and thin and striking.

'Come on then, you two. Shopping time,' I say.

'Do you really want plasticine, Ellie?' Nadine asks, linking arms.

I wish *I* was made out of plasticine. Then I'd roll myself out, long and very very thin. I'd stretch my stubby fingers into elegant manicured hands, I'd narrow my neck and my ankles, I'd scrape huge great chunks off my bottom, I'd pull off all my brown wiry hair and make myself a new long blond hairstyle . . .

'Ellie?' says Nadine. 'You're dreaming.'

Yes. Dream on, Ellie.

'I don't really know what I want,' I say. 'Let's look round for a bit.'

'Shall we go and see the teddy bears?' says Magda. 'I think they're really cute.'

At Christmas time the Flowerfields Centre updates its mechanical singing teddy bear display. They sprinkle fake snow over the flowers, dress the teddies in winter woollies, turn the biggest teddy into Tubby Christmas with a red robe and a cotton wool beard, add a few parcels and presents and a glittery tree and change the tapes inside the bears. *Bananas in Pyjamas* and *Teddy Bears' Picnic* get a rest. The bears let rip with *Jingle Bells*. They jingle those bells over and over and over again.

'I had to stand in front of those bloody bears for

over half an hour last time I was here with Eggs,' I say. 'I can't take any more torture, Magda.'

'At least Eggs doesn't dance to the music,' says Nadine. 'Natasha waits till she's got a good audience and then points her toes and flits about. It's the most utterly emetic sight ever.'

'You're a couple of sour old bats. I want to see the teddies,' says Magda. She puts her chin down and pouts. 'Me want to see the *teddies*!'

'You *look* like a bloody teddy in your new jacket, Magda,' I say. 'Watch out the Flowerfields people don't plonk you down beside Tubby Christmas and make you sing *Rudolph the Red-nosed Reindeer*.'

But we let Magda hover around the Bear Pit for a couple of verses just to show willing. Nadine starts yawning and wanders off.

'Hey, what's going on? Up on the top floor?'

She's looking up past the fountains and bubble lifts and the giant Christmas tree to the top-floor balcony. I peer short-sightedly behind my glasses. There are crowds of people up there in a long queue.

'They'll be waiting to see Father Christmas – the real one.'

'You believe in Father Christmas, Ellie? How sweet,' says Magda, tapping her foot and clicking her fingers to *Jingle Bells*.

'The guy dressed up as opposed to the singing teddy,' I say.

'They're a bit old for Father Christmas, aren't they?' says Magda. 'They're girls our age. Lots and lots of them.'

15

A light keeps flashing up there, and an excited buzz circles the atrium.

'Is it television?' says Nadine.

'Wow, I hope so,' says Magda, adjusting her furry jacket and fluffing her hair. 'Come on, let's go and see for ourselves.'

There are too many people waiting for the bubble lifts so we go on the giant escalator. As we get nearer the top I start to focus. There're hundreds of teenage girls milling about up there, and big banners everywhere with the *Spicy* logo.

'*Spicy*, the magazine,' says Magda. 'Are they doing a special promotion? I hope they're giving out free goodies. Come on, you two, let's get in the queue quick.'

She dashes up the last stretch of the escalator, her patent boots shining.

'Come on, Ellie,' says Nadine, starting to run too.

'I think *Spicy* sucks,' I say. 'I don't really want any of their freebies.'

'Then you can use them for Christmas presents, right?' says Nadine.

So the three of us join the queue. It's so jam-packed and jostling that we have to hang on hard to each other. It's horribly hot at the top of the building. Magda unbuttons her jacket and fans her face. Nadine's ghostly pallor pinkens.

'Maybe this isn't such a great idea,' I say.

I'm squashed up so close to the girl in front of me that her long silky hair veils my face. Everyone's so much taller than me. I try craning my neck but the

16

nearer we get to the front the harder it is to see what's going on. Lights keep on flashing and every now and then there's a squeal, but they're playing such loud rock music it's hard to hear what anyone's saying.

'Magda?' I tug her furry sleeve, but she's bouncing away to the music and doesn't respond.

'Nadine?' She's tall enough to see – and she's staring, transfixed.

'*What's happening?*' I yell at her.

She shouts something about a competition.

'Do we have to go in for it?' I say, sighing.

I don't think I'll be any good at a *Spicy* competition. I don't know much about music. I don't even bother reading *NME*. Nadine will do much better than me. Or maybe it's a fashion competition. I still haven't got a clue. Magda talks designer labels like they're all personal friends of hers but I don't even know how to pronounce the Italian ones, and I can never work out what all those initials stand for.

'Let's go and shop,' I beg, but there's a little surge forward, and suddenly Magda shoves hard, tugging us along after her.

We're almost at the front. I blink in the bright lights. There are huge *Spicy* posters and lots of promotion girls in pink T-shirts rushing round taking everyone's names and addresses. Each girl goes up in turn to a backdrop and stands there looking coy while a photographer clicks his camera.

There's a very pretty girl having her photo taken now: long hair, huge eyes, skinny little figure. She poses with one thumb hooked casually in her jeans.

17

She pouts her lips just like a real model.

The next girl's really stunning too. I look round. They all are. And then at long last the penny drops.

This is a *modelling* competition!

'Oh my God!' I gasp.

Magda darts forward and claims her turn. She takes off her jacket and slings it over one shoulder, her other hand fluffing up her bright blond hair. She smiles, her lipstick glossy, her teeth white.

She looks good. She may be too small, but she looks really cute, really sexy.

'Wow, get Magda,' I say to Nadine. 'Come on, let's get *out* of here.'

But Nadine is still staring. I pull her. She doesn't budge.

'Nadine, please! They'll think *we're* going in for this model competition crap,' I say.

'Well. We might as well have a go, eh?' says Nadine.

'What?'

'It'll be a laugh,' says Nadine, and she rushes forward to give her name to a girl in pink.

I watch Nadine stand in front of the camera. It's suddenly like I'm watching a stranger. I've always known Magda is seriously sexy and attractive. She looked pretty stunning at eleven that first day I sat next to her at secondary school. But I've known Nadine most of my life. She's more like my sister than my friend. I've never really *looked* at her.

I look at her now. She stands awkwardly, not smiling, with none of Magda's confidence. She's not really *pretty*. But I can see the girls in pink are taking a real interest in her, and the photographer asks her to turn while he takes several photos.

Her long hair looks so black and glossy, her skin so eerily pale. She's so tall, with her slender neck and beautiful hands and long long legs. And she's so thin. Model-girl thin.

'You're next. Name?' says a pink T-shirt, shoving a clipboard in my face.

'What? No! Not me,' I stammer, and I turn and try to elbow my way back through the huge queue.

'Watch it!'

'Hey, stop shoving.'

'What's her problem, eh?'

'Surely *she* doesn't think she could make it as a model? She's far too fat!'

Too fat, too fat, too fat.

Too F-A-T!

# Chapter Two

## Elephantgirl

# Elephantgirl

I run to get out of the Centre. I want to run right out of myself. I'm surrounded by all these perfect pretty posing girls. I'm waddling way down at their slender waist-level, the dumpy fat freak.

'Ellie! Hang on! Where are you going?'

'Wait for us!'

Magda and Nadine are chasing after me. I can't escape. I've got tears in my eyes. Oh God. I blink and blink.

'Ellie, what's up?' Magda says, catching hold of me.

'Are you *crying*?' Nadine says, putting her arm round me.

'Of course not. I just needed some air. It was so hot crammed together like that. I felt faint. Sick. I still do.'

Magda backs away a little, getting her new furry jacket out of vomit-range.

'Let's go to the Ladies room,' says Nadine. 'We'll get you a drink of water.'

'You haven't gone white,' says Magda. 'In fact, exactly the opposite. And what a shame you missed your turn to be photographed.'

'We can always go back and queue up again,' says Nadine.

'No thanks!' I say. 'I didn't *want* a turn. I didn't have any idea it was for a crappy competition. I mean, who wants to be a model?' My voice cracks. I don't think I'm convincing either of them.

'Oh yes, it would be such an ordeal!' says Magda. 'Think of all the money, the fame, the travel, the super clothes . . . *dreadful*! God, Ellie, don't be so stupid.'

'Lay off her, Magda, she's not feeling well,' says Nadine. 'Anyway, it's not like we've got any chance. There were heaps and heaps of really gorgeous-looking girls having a go.'

'Yeah, I reckon half of them were semi-professional anyway, which isn't fair,' says Magda.

They natter on about it endlessly. I listen hard when I go in the loo. Are they whispering about me? Are they raising their eyebrows and shaking their heads over poor plain plump Ellie? My eyes smart. Tears spurt down my cheeks and I have to take off my glasses and dab my face dry with loo-roll. I don't want to come out and face them. I don't want to face anyone ever again.

I could be Ellie the reclusive loo-squatter. I could set up home in this tiny cubicle. It could be quite cosy if I had a sleeping-bag and my sketch pad and a pile of books. In medieval times troubled young girls locked themselves away in tiny cells in churches and no-one thought it strange at all. Nowadays there might be an initial flurry of media interest: THE LASS LOCKED IN THE LADIES . . . SCHOOL-GIRL ELLIE STAYS SITTING ON THE LOO FOR THIRD DAY RUNNING! But eventually people would take it for granted that the end cubicle on the right in the Flowerfields Shopping Centre Ladies room is permanently engaged.

'Ellie, are you all right?'

'What are you *doing* in there?'

I have to come out. I try to chat as if I'm perfectly OK. I traipse all round the shopping centre looking for Christmas presents. It's no use. I can't make up my mind about anything. I could buy Magda the red knickers and Nadine the black, tiny wisps of under-wear, size small. They wouldn't fit me. I am not medium. Soon I won't even be large. I shall be outsize. Ellie the Elephant size.

I keep catching glimpses of myself in windows and mirrors. I seem to be getting squatter by the second. Magda drags us into *Stuck on You*, this new ultra-hip clothes shop that's just opened at the Flowerfields Shopping Centre. It's agony. I'm surrounded by skimpy little garments, skirts that would barely fit round one of my thighs, halter tops I'd have to wear as bangles. The assistants are staring at us. There's a six-stone girl dressed in black with short white hair and rings in her nose and navel, and a slender black guy with a diamond earstud in a tight white T-shirt to show off his toned body.

'Let's go,' I beg.

But Magda is eyeing up the boy and wants to try stuff on. Nadine is gazing enviously at the clothes and is happy to hang around too. So I have to wait for them both, feeling more and more like a guinea pig in a ferret's cage.

'Don't you want to try anything on too?' the white-haired girl asks.

That's what she says, but she's smirking as she says it. It's as if she's underlining the fact that nothing in the shop would fit me anyway.

'Hey, Nadine, Magda,' I hiss through the changing-room curtain. 'I'm going home, OK?'

'What? Oh, Ellie, don't go all moody,' says Magda. 'We'll only be a minute. Can you ask that guy if he's got these jeans in another size?'

'You ask him. I really have to go.'

'Are you feeling sick again, Ellie?' asks Nadine.

'Yes. I want to go home.'

'Well, wait, and we'll *take* you home,' says Nadine.

'I can't wait,' I say, and I make a run for it.

They're still in their underwear so they can't come after me. I rush through the Flowerfields Centre. Up at the top the lights are still flashing and the queue is even bigger and all around me there are girls much taller than me, much prettier than me, much much much thinner than me.

I really do feel sick. It's no better when I'm out in the open air. The bus going home lurches so much I

25

have to get off several stops early. I walk through the streets yawning with nausea. I catch sight of myself in a car window. Yawning-Hippo Girl.

Thank God there's no-one at home. Dad has taken Eggs swimming. Anna's gone up to London to have lunch with some old schoolfriend. I go straight upstairs to my room and throw myself on my bed. The springs groan under my great weight. I rip my glasses off and bury my head in the pillow, ready for a long howl. I've been fighting back tears for hours but now I can cry in peace they won't come. I just make silly snivelling noises that sound so stupid I shut up.

I roll over onto my back. I feel my body with my hands. They mountaineer up each peak and descend each valley. I pinch my waist viciously to see if I can grab a whole handful of fat but my clothes get in the way. I unbutton my sweater and pull it over my head. I struggle up off the bed. I remove everything else. I can see my reflection in the wardrobe mirror but it's just a pink blur. I put on my glasses.

It's like I'm looking at my own body for the first time. I look at my round face with its big baby cheeks and double chin, I look at my balloon breasts, I look at my flabby waist, I look at my saggy soft stomach, I look at my vast wobbly bum, I look at my massive thighs, I look at my round arms and blunt elbows, I look at my dimpled knees and thick ankles, I look at my plump padded feet.

I stand there, feeling like I've stepped into a science-fiction movie. An alien has invaded my body and blown it up out of all recognition.

I can't believe I'm so fat. I've always known I'm a bit chubby. Plump. Biggish. But not *fat*.

I whisper the word. I think of greasy swamps of chip fat stagnating in the pan. I look at my body and see the lard beneath the skin. I start clawing at myself, as if I'm trying to rip the flesh right off me.

The girl in the mirror now looks crazy as well as fat. I turn away quickly and pull my clothes back on. My jeans feel so tight I can barely do up the zip. My sweater strains obscenely over my breasts. I brush my hair to try to cover my great moon face. I keep having one more look at myself to see if I might have changed in the last two seconds. I look worse each time.

I've never exactly *liked* the way I look. I suppose it was different when I was a little kid. I can remember my mum brushing my wild curls into two big bunches and tying them with bright ribbons, scarlet one day, emerald green the next. 'You look so cute, Ellie,' she'd say, and I *felt* cute. Maybe I even *was* cute in my dungarees and stripy T-shirts and bright boots to match the ribbons. I was cuddly, that was all. I was definitely cute, with my happy hairstyle and big dark eyes and dimples.

But then my mum died. Everything changed. I changed too. I felt empty all the time so I couldn't stop eating: doughnuts and sticky buns and chocolate and toffees. The sourer I felt inside the more I had to stuff myself with sweets. So I got much fatter, and then Dad noticed I frowned whenever I read and I

27

had to wear glasses and Anna my new stepmother tried to dress me in conventional little-girly outfits that made me look like a piglet in a party frock.

I knew this but somehow I still stayed *me* inside. I could still *act* cute. People still liked me at school. They thought me funny. They wanted to be my friend. Even at Anderson High School I still fitted in. I wasn't the most popular girl in the class, I wasn't the cleverest, I wasn't the most stylish or streetwise, I didn't come top in anything apart from Art. But I was still one of the OK Girls. I wasn't a swot, I wasn't a slag, I wasn't a baby, I wasn't covered in spots, I wasn't fat. Not *really* fat, like poor Alison Smith in our year, at least fifteen stone, waddling slowly up and down the corridors as if she were wading through water, her eyes little glints inside the huge padded cage of her head.

I give a little gasp. Another stare in the mirror. I know it's mad but I'm suddenly starting to wonder if I'm actually as fat as Alison. *Fatter??*

If I don't watch out I could become an Alison. I'm going on a diet. I'm going on a diet right this minute.

It's lunchtime. Magda and Nadine will be sitting in the ice cream parlour sharing a chicken club sandwich with crisps and little gherkins, and sipping huge frothy strawberry sodas.

My tummy rumbles.

'Shut up,' I say. I punch myself hard in my own stomach. 'You're not getting fed today, do you hear, you great big ugly gut?'

It hears but it doesn't understand. It gurgles and

complains and aches. I try not to pay it any attention. I get out my sketch pad and draw myself in elephantine guise and then I pin the picture above my bed.

Then I draw myself the way I really want to be. Well, I *want* to be five foot eight with long straight blonde hair and big blue eyes, only there's no way this could ever happen. No, I draw myself the way I *could* be if I only stuck to a proper diet. Still small. Still frizzy-haired. Still bespectacled. But thin.

I wonder how long it will take. I'd like to lose a couple of stones at *least*. I went on this diet once before. It was all Magda's idea. The aim was to lose a couple of pounds a week. It's not going to be quick enough. I can't stand being so fat. I want to change *now*. If only I could unzip myself from chin to crotch and step out of my old self, sparklingly slim.

I wonder if Magda will go on a diet with me again? She was useless last time, she only managed a couple of days. So I gave up too. But then Magda doesn't really need to lose much weight at all. A few pounds and she'd be perfect. And as for Nadine . . .

I think of her standing there at the *Spicy* magazine competition, effortlessly, elegantly skinny. I don't know what I think about it. I'm pleased because Nadine's my oldest friend. I'm envious because I'd love to be that thin. And I'm angry because it's so unfair. Nadine often eats more than me. I've seen her eat two Mars bars on the trot. OK, she often skips meals too, but it's not deliberate, she just forgets because she isn't always hungry.

Not like me. I am *ravenous*. I hear Dad and Eggs

come back from swimming. There's a lot of chatter down in the kitchen. And then this smell. It wafts under my bedroom door, over to my bed, up into each nostril. Oh my God, Dad's frying bacon, they're having bacon sandwiches. I *love* bacon sandwiches. Dad's not that great at cooking but he does wonderful bacon sandwiches, toasting the bread and spreading it with great puddles of golden butter and crisping the bacon until there are no slimy fatty bits . . .

'Hey, can I have a bacon sandwich?' my mouth shouts before I can stop it.

I hurtle downstairs. Dad looks surprised to see me.

'I thought you were out somewhere with Nadine and Magda?'

I don't have to conjure up some convincing explanation because Eggs starts talking non-stop.

'I dived in, Ellie, a real dive, well, the first time was a sort of fall, I didn't really mean to do it, but then Dad said go for it, Eggs, that wasn't a fall it was a dive, so I dived again, I dived lots, guess what, I can dive . . .'

'Big deal,' I say, breathing in the bacon smell.

I can scarcely wait. I want to snatch it direct from the frying pan.

'*You* can't dive, Ellie, not like me. *I* can dive. I'm a good diver, aren't I, Dad?'

'Sure, little Eggs, the best. Though Ellie can dive too.'

'No, she can't!' Eggs insists, outraged.

'Can can can,' I say childishly.

30

'You can't, because you don't ever go swimming,' says Eggs, with six-year-old logic.

'She used to be a cracking little swimmer once,' says Dad, surprisingly. 'Remember when we used to go, Ellie? Hey, why don't you come one Saturday with Eggs and me?'

'Yes, then I can show you how I can dive. I bet you *can't* dive, well, not the way I can. I want the first bacon sandwich, Dad! *Dad*! *I* want the first one!'

'Pipe down, Mr Bossy,' says Dad, and he hands the sandwich over to me.

It's not often I get put before Eggs. I smile at Dad, and then wonder if he's just feeling sorry for me. Maybe all that snivelling has left my eyes puffy. In my great big piggy face.

I look at my bacon sandwich sizzling in splendour on the blue willow pattern plate. I pick it up, and it's still so hot I can hardly hold it. I raise it to my lips. There's a little fold of bacon poking out of the toast, glistening with goodness.

No, not goodness. Badness. Fat. To make *me* fat. How many calories are there in a bacon sandwich? I don't know, but it must be heaps. If I eat pig I'll turn into a pig, a great big swollen-bellied porker. I imagine myself a vast sow wallowing in muck – and I put the sandwich back on the plate.

'Here, Eggs, you have it if it means so much to you.'

'*Really*?' says Eggs, astonished. He takes a big bite immediately in case I change my mind.

'Well, you have this one, Ellie,' says Dad.

31

'I'm not really hungry, actually,' I say. 'In fact I feel a bit sick. Maybe it's the smell of the bacon. I think I'll go up to my room.'

'Ellie? I *thought* you looked a bit odd. I hope you haven't got some dreaded bug,' says Dad.

I go upstairs, my tummy feeling like a huge cavern, my mouth slavering like a waterfall with that glorious smell.

I want a bacon sandwich so *much*. Just *one* won't hurt.

No. Think pig. Big big big pig.

I draw an Ellie pig upstairs. I start on an entire menagerie of Outsize Ellie Animals. Ellie warty warthog. Ellie snaggle-tooth rhino. Ellie blubbery seal. Ellie humpback whale.

I hear the phone downstairs and then Dad calling. It's Nadine.

I don't want to talk to Nadine just now.

'Tell her I'm not feeling very well. I'll call her back.'

I hear Dad muttering. Then he calls again. 'She wants to come round to see you, OK?'

'*No!*'

I jump up, hurtle downstairs, and snatch the phone from Dad as he's about to put it down.

'Nadine?'

'Oh, Ellie. What *is* it? You just ran off!' There's a buzz behind her. She's obviously still out.

'Yeah. I'm sorry. I've just got this bug or something. I feel sick.'

'You're sure that's what it is? It's not that

we've done something to upset you?'

'No, of course not.'

'Magda thought it might be the modelling thing. She said you seemed fine before that.'

'Well, Magda's talking rubbish,' I snap. 'Let me speak to her.'

'No, she's gone off too,' says Nadine. 'We went to the Soda Fountain, right, and there were these boys and they were all going on somewhere else and they asked us too and I didn't want to go but Magda did.'

'I get the picture.'

'So can I come round to your place, Ellie? I know you don't feel very well but you can just loll on your bed and take it easy if you want.'

'Well,' I say, weakening.

'And I need your advice. You see this photographer guy, you know, the *Spicy* one, he told me he reckoned I was really in with a chance, and he said they'd be getting in touch with all the possibles quite soon and we'd have to go to this new photo session in a proper studio, and I don't know what clothes to wear, whether to go dead casual in jeans or whether they expect you to dress up in all sorts of fashion stuff. And then there's make-up. Do you think Magda would do it for me because she's much better at that sort of thing? And what about my hair? Do you think the ends need cutting, Ellie? *Ellie?* Are you still there?'

'Mmm. Nadine, I really do feel sick. Don't come round, eh? I'll phone you tomorrow. Bye.'

I can't stand to listen to Nadine another second. She's obviously getting in a twitch about nothing.

33

This photographer probably says that to all the girls. And there were so many pretty ones there today. Lots of them were heaps prettier than Nadine. She won't get chosen. She won't get to be a *Spicy* cover girl.

Oh, God, what's the matter with me? Nadine's my best friend. I *want* her to get chosen.

No, I don't.

I do. And I don't.

I can't stand feeling like this. Jade-green with jealousy.

I creep back to my room, feeling like I'm covered in shameful green slime. I don't feel like drawing any more. I try to find something to read. Mrs Madley, our English teacher, said we've all got to read *Jane Eyre* over the Christmas holidays. Everyone's outraged and says how can they possibly plough through such a huge long boring book. I moaned too, of course. Catch me letting on that I've already read it for fun. I liked the video of it so I thought I'd see what the book was like. Anna's got an old Penguin copy.

Maybe I'll get stuck into *Jane Eyre* again. Perhaps I'd better try to be as highbrow as possible seeing as I'm so hideous. And it's a good story. Jane's OK. At least she's not pretty.

I read and read and read. It's fine at first. I like all the little-girl-Jane bits because she's so fierce and then when she's sent away to school and starving all the time I identify totally. My tummy's rumbling so crazily I'd wolf down Jane's bowl of burnt porridge, no problem. Though porridge is ever so fattening, isn't it?

That's the trouble. Jane might be plain but she's this skinny little thing. People go on about it all the time. I start to get irritated. What's she got to grouch about if she's tiny? And Mr Rochester loves her. Why can't they both shut up about the first mad wife up in the attic? I skip forward to find the bit where mad Bertha growls and bites. My heart starts thumping as I read the description. She's not just hairy and purple. She's got bloated features. It says she's *corpulent*, as big as her husband. Rochester says is it any wonder that he wants Jane. He asks them to compare Jane's form with Bertha's *bulk*.

He doesn't want Bertha because she's fat. And mad. But maybe she only went mad because Rochester didn't fancy her any more when she started getting fat.

Maybe Dan won't fancy me.

Well, I don't fancy him. I mean, he's OK, he's funny, he's my friend, we sometimes fool around together – but he's just too odd and geeky and immature to be a real *boyfriend*.

He's never seen things that way. He's been nuts on me ever since we met in the summer. He's travelled down from Manchester to stay with me and he writes heaps of letters and he phones every now and then just to say hello.

I suddenly run downstairs and start dialling.

'You OK now, Ellie?' Dad calls. He's sprawling on the sofa with a can of beer. Eggs is sitting on Dad's stomach, sipping Coke. They're both dipping into a big bowl of crisps, watching football on the telly.

I think of a salty golden crisp cracking inside my mouth. Water oozes over my tongue. I'm so *hungry*.

'You ready for something to eat yet?' Dad says, proffering the crisp bowl.

'No, thanks,' I say, turning my back.

One crisp would be fatal. Then there'd be another and another until I'd munched the lot *and* licked round the bowl for the crumbs.

The phone rings for ages at Dan's house. Then one of his even geekier brothers answers. He starts waffling some nonsense about Dan being otherwise engaged. At last Dan comes to the phone himself.

'Hi! It's me.'

'Hi,' says Dan.

There is a little silence. I thought he'd act more thrilled. I've never phoned him up before, it's always him phoning me.

'What was your brother wittering on about?'

'Oh, nothing. You know what he's like.' Dan sounds awkward. 'What are you phoning for, Ellie?'

'Just to say hello.'

'Right. Well. Hello.'

I wait. There's a long pause.

'Well, can't you say something else?' I say.

'You're not saying anything either.'

I don't usually have to. He's the one who burbles nineteen to the dozen. I can't normally get a word in edgeways. But the edges are wide open now.

'What have you been up to?' I say limply.

'Well, right now I'm watching the match on television.'

'What, football? Are Man U playing?'

'*Rugby.*'

'*What?* Rugby? You hate rugby. *Everyone* hates rugby.'

'I've got quite interested recently. It's a great game actually.'

There's a distant roar his end of the phone.

'Oh nuts. I've missed a try,' says Dan.

'Don't let me keep you then,' I say sharply, and I slam down the phone.

# Chapter Three

# Greatartgirl

I can't sleep. I lie on my back and think f-o-o-d. If I
breathe in deeply I can still smell the takeaway pizza
they had for supper. Dad ate a good half of it. Eggs
nibbled the topping and the crusty bits. Anna went
without, saying she'd eaten a lot with her friend. And
I said I still felt sick.

I feel sick now. Sick with hunger. My tummy is
like a geyser, gurgling endlessly. I'm so hungry it
hurts. I groan as I toss and turn. I feel like a baby bird
with its beak gaping, cheeping non-stop. Think
cuckoo. Great big blobby baby cuckoo, twice as big
as the other birds, far fatter than the frantic step-parent
feeding it. That's me, that's Anna.

I'm sick of her being so much skinnier than me.
I'm sick of being Nadine and Magda's fat dumpy
friend. I'm sick of being fat. I'm sick. *Think* sick to

stop yourself eating. I've got to lose so much weight, I've got to get thin, I've got to, *I've got to . . .*

I'm out of bed, running barefoot down the stairs, into the kitchen, where's the pizza box? I thought there was a huge great slice left. Oh, God, did Anna dump it straight in the dustbin, no, here it is, oh, food, food, food!

The pizza is cold and congealed but I don't care. I bolt it down, barely stopping to chew, tearing off great chunks. I even eat the bits that Eggs has licked. I run my finger round the box. I get a carton of milk from the fridge and wash it all down so quickly that milk dribbles down my nightie but I'm still not satisfied. I feel hungrier than ever.

I go to the bread bin and make myself a jam sandwich, then another, then another, then a spoonful of jam by itself, more, more . . . Now, what else is there? Frosties! I eat them straight out of the packet, scooping them up in my hand, and there's sultanas too, I'm cramming so many into my mouth I nearly choke. I cough and a disgusting slurp of sultanas dribbles down my chin. I catch sight of myself in the shiny kettle and I can't believe what I look like. Total crazy woman. Oh, God, what am I doing? What have I eaten? I can *feel* the food going down into my stomach. It's starting to hurt. What am I going to do?

I run to the downstairs loo by the back door. I crouch over the toilet. I try to make myself sick. I heave and heave but I can't do it. I shove a finger in my mouth. It's horrible, oh, my stomach, two fingers,

I've got to, I've got to . . . oh . . . oooooh . . .

I am so sick. So horribly revoltingly disgustingly sick, *slowly* – again and again and again. I have to hang on to the edge of the toilet to stop myself falling. Tears stream down my face, sweat runs down my back. I pull the chain and then try to get up, the room spinning round me. My throat burns and my mouth stays sour no matter how many times I swill it with water.

'Ellie?' It's Anna in her blue pyjamas, her pageboy hair ruffled, so she only looks about my age. 'Oh you poor thing. Have you been very sick?'

'Mmm.'

'Come here, let's get you sorted out.' She puts the lid down on the loo and makes me sit on it. Then she runs the towel under the tap and gently mops my face and hair as if I were Eggs. I lean against her weakly and she puts her arm around me.

This is weird. Anna and I are acting like a regular mother and daughter. We never ever act like this. I made it quite plain right from the start when she came to live with us that I didn't want another mum. I *had* a mum, even if she was dead. For years I wouldn't let Anna near me. We didn't exactly *fight* – we were just like two strangers forced to live under the same roof. Just recently we've started to get a bit closer. We go shopping together or we watch a video or we flick through a glossy magazine but it's just like sisters. Big sister, little sister. Well. I'm bigger than Anna. Not taller. *Fatter.* It's so unfair. Why do I have to be fatter than everyone?

Tears are still running down my cheeks.

'Hey,' says Anna gently, wiping my eyes. 'Do you feel really terrible, Ellie?'

'Yes,' I say mournfully.

'Have you got a bad tummy-ache? Headache?' Anna puts her hand on my forehead. 'I wonder if you've got a temperature? Maybe I should call the doctor?'

'No! No, I'm OK. I was just sick, that's all. Probably just something I ate!'

'You're still ever so white. And you're shivering.' Anna leads me into the kitchen and gets her old denim jacket that's hanging on the back door. 'Here.' She wraps it round me and sits me down at the kitchen table. 'Do you want a drink of water?'

I sip it delicately.

'Your dad said you've been feeling lousy all day, not eating anything.' Anna sighs. 'I wish I could say the same for him. Look at the state of the kitchen! He must have had a secret midnight feast – and then he moans because his jeans won't do up!'

'Why does he still try to squeeze himself into those jeans anyway,' I say, feeling guilty that Dad's getting the blame.

'He just won't admit that he's too fat,' says Anna, sticking everything back in the food cupboard.

'I'm even fatter,' I say, the glass clinking against my teeth.

'What? Don't be silly,' says Anna.

'I *am*. And I didn't even realize. I mean, I knew it, but it didn't really bug me. But now . . .'

'Oh Ellie. You're *not* fat. You're just . . . rounded.

It suits you. It's the way you're supposed to be.'

'I don't want to be fat, I want to be thin. As thin as you.'

'*I'm* not thin,' says Anna, though she looks like a little pin person in her schoolboy pyjamas. 'I wore my old black leather trousers today because they're about the only sexy garment I've got nowadays and I was so desperate not to look dull and mumsy and suburban, but the zip's so tight now I could barely *breathe*. It was cutting into my stomach all through lunch. Which was *not* a success. Oh God, Ellie, this friend of mine, Sara, she looks incredible. She's got this fantastic new hairstyle, all blond highlights, and the *shoes* she was wearing, really high, and the way she walked in them! Every man in the restaurant was staring at her.'

'Yes, but you don't want to look like some blond bimbo,' I say.

'But she's *not* a bimbo, she's the top designer for this new fashion chain. They're even going to be bringing out her own label, Sara Star. She showed me the logo, two big Ss in shocking pink. Oh, Ellie, she's really made it big now. She kept politely asking me what I'm doing and I had to say I haven't even got a job at the moment.'

'You've got Eggs to look after.'

'Yes, but it's not like he's a baby.'

'And Dad.'

'OK, he *is* a baby,' says Anna, smiling at last. 'But even so . . . I just feel . . . Anyway, I'm going to try even harder to find some work, even if it's just part–time. And I'm going to do something with my stupid hair. *And* I'm going to go on a diet.'

'I'm going on a diet too,' I say.

'Oh, Ellie. Look, you're still a growing girl.'

'Exactly. Growing fatter and fatter.'

'Well, we'll see when you're better. I do hope you haven't got gastric flu. It sounded as if you were being so terribly sick.'

'I'm fine now. Really. I'm going back to bed.'

'Ellie? You're acting sort of funny.' Anna looks at me worriedly. 'You would tell me if . . . if there was anything really wrong, wouldn't you?'

'*Yes.*'

Well, no. I can't tell Anna my throat is raw and my stomach still heaving because I've eaten half the food in the cupboard and then practically clawed it out of my insides with my own hand. What sort of mad revolting loony would she take me for?

I go back to bed and pull the covers right over my head. I remember this game I played when I was little, after my mum died. I'd kid myself that when it was morning I'd wake up in a different parallel life and Mum would be sitting on the end of the bed smiling at me. It was years before I gave up on that game. But now I catch myself playing a new version. No Mum. No Ellie either. Not the old one. I'll wake up and I'll get out of bed and pull off my nightie and then I'll peel off all my extra pounds too and there I'll be, new little skinny Ellie.

The old huge fat Ellie sleeps late and slouches to the bathroom in the morning. I can smell faint eggy

45

toasty smells. Oh, God. I hope they've all finished eating when I come down.

Dad is on his third coffee and delve-into-the biscuit-tin stage. Eggs is busy making some kind of collage with macaroni and what's left of the sultanas. I can't look at them without feeling sick.

'Toast, Ellie?' says Anna.

'No thanks. Just coffee. Black,' I say quickly.

'Look at my lovely picture, Ellie, *look*,' says Eggs.

'You *still* not well, chum? Anna said you were horribly sick in the night,' says Dad.

'I'm OK. I just don't fancy anything to eat yet.'

'Are you sure?'

'Mmm. Maybe I'll go back to bed in a bit, OK?' It'll be easier avoiding food upstairs. And if I can sleep I won't be feeling so starving hungry all the time.

'Well, we were planning on eating out at lunch-time and then maybe having a little jaunt somewhere,' says Dad.

'To see some pictures, Dad says,' says Eggs. 'Look at *my* picture, Ellie. See what it is?'

'Yes, macaroni and sultanas, very fetching,' I say. 'You lot go out. That's fine with me. I'll just flop around.'

'But I haven't got any food in for your lunch, Ellie,' says Anna. 'I missed out on the big Saturday shop because I was seeing Sara.'

'I'll cook myself some eggs or something. It's OK,' I say.

'It's a *lady*, Ellie, can't you see? The macaroni is all

46

her *curls*, and the sultanas are her eyes and her nose and her smiley mouth, see.'

'Well, she's got a dirty nose and very black teeth and she's having a seriously bad hair day,' I say.

'Don't be mean to him,' says Dad, giving me a little nudge. 'Come out with us, eh? You'll feel better for a bit of fresh air.'

'No, thanks.'

Nadine rings around twelve, pained that I haven't phoned her back. She wants to come round this afternoon and she's still burbling about her hair and her make-up and her clothes in case she gets selected as a *Spicy* cover girl.

'Nadine! Look, wait till they get in touch with you, right?' I'm not quite bitchy enough to add 'Maybe they won't' but I imply it.

'I want to be *prepared*, Ellie. *Please* can I come round?' Nadine lowers her voice. 'My gran and grandad are here and this Happy Families lark is getting way too heavy for me. They're all gathered round Natasha just *watching* her, as if she's a little television set or something, and my God, is she performing with her volume turned right up.'

'Oh, Nad,' I say, weakening. 'Look, I don't know what help *I* can be. I'm no expert when it comes to make-up and stuff. Why don't you go and see Magda?'

I expect Nadine to say that she and I are best friends from way back and that she wants to plan it all with me. Then I'll swallow the last sour jealousy pill and ask her over and fuss round her like a real friend. I'll try terribly hard not to mind that she's got serious model girl potential, and I'm just her fat freaky friend.

'Oh, I've tried Magda. She's so great with make-up. I thought she'd maybe trim my hair for me too. But she's going out with this guy she met at the Soda Fountain. Not the one she really fancied, this is his friend – but life's like that. Anyway, I can come over, Ellie, can't I? Straight after lunch?'

I take a deep breath.

'Sorry, Nadine. We're going out for lunch, and then on up to town somewhere,' I say. 'See you tomorrow at school. Bye.'

'You're coming,' Dad calls from the kitchen. 'Great.'

'I wish you wouldn't listen to my phone calls. They're *private*,' I say. 'And I'm not really coming. I just said that to get out of seeing Nadine.'

'Of course you're coming,' says Dad. 'And what's up with you and Nadine? I thought you two girls were practically joined at the hip? Have you broken friends?'

'Of course not. You make us sound like little kids,' I say haughtily.

'Just don't break friends with Magda too. She's a really cracking little girl,' says Dad, with a touch too much enthusiasm.

'Stop bugging Ellie,' says Anna sharply. 'And Magda's young enough to be your daughter.'

So I end up going out with Anna and Dad and Eggs to this teashop in Clapham. It's a great place, actually, with lovely deep blue and pink decor and Lloyd Loom cushioned chairs and round glass-topped tables, and all sorts of interesting people hang out there, students, actors, huge crowds of friends or romantic couples . . . but it's not the place to go with your *parents*. I feel a total idiot, convinced everyone is staring at this sad fat girl who has no social life of her own. And the menu is agony. I read my way through all the delicious choices twice over: bacon lettuce and tomato sandwich, smoked salmon and scrambled eggs, bagels, scones with jam and cream, cheesecake, banoffee pie, sticky toffee pudding . . .

'Just a black coffee, please.'

'Isn't there *anything* you fancy, Ellie?' Dad says worriedly. 'What about chocolate fudge cake? I thought that was your favourite?'

Oh, Dad, they're all my favourites. I could easily eat my way through the entire menu. I'm almost crying with hunger as I look at everyone's piled plates.

'She's still feeling a bit queasy,' says Anna. 'But you'll have to eat something, Ellie, or you'll pass out.'

I end up agreeing to a plate of scrambled eggs. Eggs aren't too fattening, are they? Though they come with two rounds of golden toast glistening with butter. I tell myself I'll just toy with a forkful of egg – but within five minutes my plate looks as if it's licked clean.

'There! Great, you've obviously got your appetite back,' Dad says happily. 'So how about a wicked cake too?'

'Yes, I want cake, Dad,' says Eggs, although he has only nibbled his prawn sandwich. He pulls out every prawn and puts them in a circle on his plate.

'Eat them *up*, Eggs,' says Anna.

'They don't want to be eaten! They want to have a swim round my plate, don't you, little pink prawnies?' says Eggs. He's playing up to his audience in sickening fashion.

'All those little prawns want to swim in your tummy, Eggs,' says Dad. 'Open your mouth and I'll make them dive in.'

'Oh please. He's not a *baby*,' I hiss.

I have to sit through this entire performance and then watch while Eggs is rewarded with a strawberry mountain cake. He eats the strawberries and leaves the mountain of cream after one or two token licks. I want to snatch it up and gobble it down. I have to clench my fist to stop my hand reaching out. I think of myself as a mountain with little strawberry blobs in appropriate places and manage to resist.

Anna sips her coffee without obvious envy. Dad wolfs down a whacking great slice of banana cake with no inhibition whatsoever. His shirt buttons are straining, his belly bulging over the top of his jeans. He doesn't seem to care. And it's so unfair, it's different for men – women *still* seem to fancy my fat old dad. The pretty waitress in her tiny skirt has a happy little chat with him as he pays the bill. She's so skinny. Her skimpy top only just reaches her waist and as she moves you can see her beautiful flat tummy. How does she work here surrounded by all this super food and not eat?

Oh God, I'm so hungry. The scrambled eggs and toast have made me even *hungrier*. And it gets worse when we park the car near Trafalgar Square and go in the National Gallery. I don't mind art galleries but they *always* make me starving hungry, especially after the first fifteen minutes when I'm starting to get bored.

I get bored very quickly today. Eggs is being ultra-exasperating, asking endless idiotic questions.

'Who is that funny little baby?'

'Why does that pretty lady in blue have that gold plate round her head?'

'I can see the donkey and the cow but why don't they have any pigs and chickens on their farm?'

All the people in the gallery smile at him. Dad explains, going into great long rigmaroles although Eggs isn't really listening. Anna pats him on the head and picks him up to show him special things.

I pretend I'm going round the gallery by myself. The paintings start to soothe me. I stand for ages in front of a serious pale woman in a sumptuous green velvet dress sitting on the floor engrossed in a book. I feel as if I'm being sucked right into the painting . . . but then I'm dragged off to another part of the gallery and Eggs starts his little act again.

He clasps his hands and pops his eyes at a painting called *The Origin of the Milky Way*.

'Ooooh! Look at that lady! Isn't she *rude*?' he pipes.

I sigh. Anna shushes. Dad tells Eggs that it isn't rude at all, not when it's a great painter illustrating an extra-ordinary myth.

'*I* think she's rude,' says Eggs. 'She is rude, isn't she, Ellie?'

I find the painting a bit embarrassing myself but I affect a lofty air.

'You're just too young to appreciate great art, Eggs,' I say.

'No, I'm not. I *like* the art. I just think it's rude. That lady's got wobbly bits just like *you*.'

I know he just means breasts, any shape or size. But the word wobbly still makes me want to burst into tears. I feel myself going hot. A bright pink wobbly blancmange.

'I'll meet you lot at the entrance in half an hour, right?' I say, and I shove off quickly by myself.

The word wobbly wiggles around my brain like a great worm. I try to absorb myself in the art now I'm on my own but it doesn't work. I find I'm just staring desperately at every painted woman to see how fat she is. It's hard to tell with all the virgins because their blue robes are voluminous.

I concentrate on the nudes. The thinnest is a languid pin-up Venus wearing a huge fancy hat, two strings of beads and nothing else. She poses sugges-tively, one arm up, one leg bent. Her beautiful long lean body makes me think of Nadine.

There's another rounder Venus kissing a very young Cupid while all sorts of strange creatures cavort in the background. She's disturbingly sexy, very aware of all her charms, not really *thin* but well-toned and taut, as if she worked out in the gym every day. She's the spitting image of Magda.

I look for myself. I don't get any further than Rubens. I look at double chins, padded arms, flabby thighs, domed stomachs, enormous dimpled bottoms. Three huge hefty women are being offered a golden apple. They look as if they eat an entire orchard of apples every day.

I am never going to eat again.

# Chapter Four

Whalegirl

# Whalegirl

So I don't eat.

I don't bite. I don't chew. I don't swallow. Simple.

Only of course it's not simple at all. It's the hardest thing ever. I think of nothing else all day long.

Breakfast is no problem. I wake so hungry that I feel weak and queasy and the sight of Dad chomping and Eggs slurping puts me off food altogether. Anna and I sip black coffee in a smug sisterly way.

School dinners are easily solved too. The smell steals along the corridors and invades the classroom and just at first my nose twitches, my stomach rumbles, and my mouth drools desperately. But it's easier actually in the canteen where the smell is overwhelming and the sight is sickening if I try hard enough. It's as if I'm wearing new lenses in my glasses. The sausages become charred penises, obscenely pink

56

where the skins are split. The pizza looks diseased, oozing bloody tomato and pus-yellow cheese. The baked potatoes steam like horse droppings. It's easy to back away.

It's far harder when Magda and Nadine offer me food. Magda presses a whole slice of her mother's home-made pecan pie on me at break and before I can contaminate it with my thoughts I have eaten it all, the sweet moistness sliding straight down my throat in seconds. It's so good I feel tears in my eyes. I've been near-starving for days and it's so wonderful easing that gnawing need inside me – and yet as soon as it's all gone and I'm left with sticky lips and crumbs on my fingers I'm horrified.

How many calories? 300? 400? Maybe 500? All that syrup, all that butter, all those wickedly fattening pecans.

I say I have to go to the cloakroom but Magda and Nadine come too, and I can't thrust my fingers down my throat and throw up because they'd hear me.

Nadine is forever nibbling at Kit Kats and Twixes. It's so unfair. *How* can she stay so skinny? And her white skin is flawless, she doesn't even get spots. She eats her chocolate bars absent-mindedly, snapping off a couple of pieces every so often and offering them to Magda and me.

'Nadine. I'm on a *diet*,' I say, brushing her hand away.

'Yeah, yeah, you and your diets, Ellie,' says Nadine.

So OK, in the past I've tried dieting, but never *seriously*. This time it's different. It has to be.

It's even harder when I get home. I'm so used to eating tea the minute I get in from school, bread and honey, oatcakes and cheese, bunches of grapes, hot chocolate, home-made shortbread – good wholesome wonderful food. No, *bad* food that bloats me into a great big wobbly blob. I can't eat it. I won't eat it.

Anna doesn't argue. She makes Eggs his own tea and we have ours: celery and carrot sticks and apple wedges. We snap and crunch briskly. Eggs wonders if he is missing out on anything. He demands a stick of celery too.

'It doesn't taste of anything,' he says, astonished. 'I don't like it.'

'We don't like it either.'

'Then you're silly to eat it,' says Eggs.

Dad thinks we're even sillier. He watches Anna and me cut our one slice of ham and quarter our one tomato and eat our way through endless lettuce leaves for supper.

'You're both nuts,' he says. 'What are you *doing*, going on this crazy diet? You're still matchstick thin, Anna – and I don't know what's got into *you*, Ellie. You've always been a girl who loves her food.'

'Meaning I've always been a fat pig so why don't I stay one?' I say, choking on my forkful of lettuce. It stays in my throat, rank moist vegetation. What am I doing trying to eat it? I spit it out into a paper hankie, shuddering.

'Yuck! Ellie spat! *I'm* not allowed to spit, am I, Mum?'

'Just be quiet, Eggs.'

'Don't do that, Ellie! I didn't *say* you were fat, for God's sake.'

'That's what you meant.'

'No, I didn't. You're *not* fat, you're . . .'

'Yes? What am I?'

'You're just . . . ordinary nice girl-size,' Dad says desperately.

'Nadine and Magda are ordinary nice girls but I'm much fatter than them, aren't I?'

'*I* don't know.'

'Of course you know! Magda's got a lovely figure. You certainly should know that, Dad, you can't keep your eyes off her when she calls round.'

'Ellie!' says Anna sharply.

'And Nadine is so thin and gorgeous she's going to be a model for *Spicy* magazine,' I shout, leaving the table.

I charge up to my room, crying. I stare at myself in my mirror, hoping I might look tragic with tears coursing down my face, but I just look blotchy. My nose is running. I have slimy green lettuce stuck to my teeth. And I'm still fat. Fat fat fat. I've hardly eaten for days and I've only lost four pounds. I stand on the scales stark naked every morning – and I strip off when I come home from school, *and* try again last thing at night. Four pounds sounds a lot when you look at two bags of sugar, but I don't know where it's come off *me*. My cheeks are still puffed out like a frog, my body still bulges, my bum wobbles, my hips spread. I feel myself swelling up all over so that the mirror can barely contain me.

It turns out it's true about Nadine. She comes waltzing into school waving a letter.

'Ellie! Magda! You'll never ever guess what!'

I guess. We guess. The whole class guesses, circling Nadine in awe.

'Are you *really* going to be a model, Nadine?'

'Well, it's just the first heat, on the nineteenth of December up in London, but they say there were heaps of girls, *thousands*, who didn't make it through to this stage.'

'Thanks, Nadine! I know my place. Bottom of the heap,' says Magda. 'Here, maybe I left home before the post came. Maybe *I'm* through to the first heat too.'

'What's going on, girls?' says Mrs Henderson, coming into the classroom. 'You're all buzzing like a hive of bees.'

'Well, we're just the drones. Nadine's the Queen Bee,' I say.

It comes out a little too sharply. I smile at Nadine to show her I'm just joking. She's so out of her head with excitement she doesn't even notice. Oh, God, she looks so beautiful. Of course she'll end up the winner.

'A cover girl on *Spicy* magazine?' says Mrs Henderson, eyebrows raised.

'Isn't Nadine *lucky*?' the class chorus.

'I'm only in the first heat,' Nadine says modestly.

'I don't think I'll ever make it. I'll be so *nervous* on the nineteenth.'

'What's happening then?' says Mrs Henderson, her hands on her hips.

'That's when I have to go to this studio in London. We all have to wear these special clothes and pose.'

'Oh Nadine! You'll actually be *modelling*.'

'Modelling,' Mrs Henderson repeats, but she puts an entirely different spin on the word. She makes it sound as if it's the last thing in the world she'd want to do. I feel a shameful stab of relief. Then I look at Mrs Henderson properly. Fat chance *she'd* ever have of being a model. Fat being the operative word. Well, she's not *fat* fat, but she's stockily built, with big muscles, and her grey sweatsuit fits a little too snugly.

'When are you intending to go to this studio, Nadine? In the evening? You will make sure this is a properly supervised modelling session, won't you? Take your mother with you,' says Mrs Henderson.

'I'm not going with my mum!' says Nadine. 'But it's OK, Mrs Henderson, it's totally respectable. There'll be heaps of other girls there – and it's in the daytime.'

'The daytime,' says Mrs Henderson. She pauses. 'Then you'll be at school.'

'It's on *Saturday*, Mrs Henderson.'

'Ah! Just as well.'

'But you'd have let me have a day off school anyway, wouldn't you, Mrs Henderson?'

'Dream on, Nadine,' says Mrs Henderson briskly. 'I shall expect you to volunteer for extra PE lessons to keep you in beautifully toned condition.'

'Dream on, Mrs Henderson,' says Nadine, a little too cheekily.

Nadine ends up tidying the sports equipment cupboard in her lunch hour. Magda and I help her out. They eat crisps and swig Coke as we coil ropes and assemble hoops and herd netballs into neat piles. I sip mineral water, first one can, then another.

'Have you turned into a camel, Ellie?' says Magda.

'What do you mean?' I say defensively, looking down at my bulging body. 'Are you saying I look like I've got humps?'

'No! I'm saying you've got a *thirst* like a camel. That's your second can, isn't it?'

'So?'

'So sorry I asked,' says Magda, pulling a face at Nadine.

'You're drinking and drinking and yet you're not eating anything,' says Nadine, thrusting her bag of crisps under my nose. '*Eat*, Ellie. A few measly little crisps aren't going to make you fat. I scoff them all the time.'

'Meaning you're the one with the thin-as-a-pin model looks and yet you can still eat crisps,' I say.

'Meaning *nothing*. What's the matter with you, Ellie? Don't be such a grump.'

'Sorry, sorry.'

I *am* sorry too. I know I'm being paranoid. I know Magda and Nadine aren't getting at me. *I'm* the one who keeps griping at them.

I grit my teeth and try hard to act normally but it's

so hard when I want to snatch handfuls of their salty golden crisps and cram them into my mouth, bagful after bagful . . . I raise my second can to my lips and drain it.

I hiccup. I feel totally water-logged, a great bloated balloon – but I still don't feel *full*. I haven't eaten since yesterday's supper, and that was only salad.

I've decided now that I'm going to stick to one meal a day until I've lost at least a stone. Six more hours to go.

I start stacking quoits energetically to divert myself. I bend and stretch . . . and then the store cupboard lurches sideways and I grab at Nadine.

'Ellie?'

'She's fainting,' says Magda.

'No, I'm not,' I mumble.

The cupboard whirls round and round, the walls closing in on me.

'Put her head between her legs,' says Magda.

'You what?' says Nadine.

'It's a recovery position, nutcase. Here, Ellie, sit down. Put your head right down too. You'll be better in a minute.'

'I'm better now,' I say.

The cupboard is still spinning, but slowly.

'Shall I go and get Mrs Henderson?' asks Nadine.

'No!'

'You're still ever so pale, Ellie.'

'I'm always pale. I just went dizzy for a minute, that's all. No big deal.'

'Well, no wonder you're going dizzy if you won't

63

eat,' says Nadine. 'You and this stupid diet.'

'Don't start that again.'

'You know the best way to lose weight?' says Magda, taking a discus in either hand and trying to flex her muscles. 'Exercise. That's what you should do, Ellie.'

'Ellie, exercise?' Nadine laughs.

We are famous for being the least sporty girls ever. But I've been privately experimenting recently. I tried doing sit-ups in my bedroom to firm up my horrible wobbly tummy, but I'm so useless at it I can only sit up at all if I wedge my toes under the chest of drawers handle. I practically pulled my toes right off – they've still got painful mauve grooves across them now.

I've also tried jogging to school, though I felt ultra stupid and hoped everyone would think I was running for a bus. I only managed to go the length of two streets before collapsing. I was so sweaty I was terrified I'd overwhelmed the efficiency of my Mum rollette and I had to keep my distance from everyone all day long.

'I know exercise is a good idea,' I say. 'It's not that I don't want to do it. I can't. You know how useless I am, Magda.'

'It's only because you're not fit,' Magda persists. 'How about going to a gym?'

'Please!' says Nadine, shaking her long locks in horror.

'Go on, Ellie, you might find it fun. There's a

special early gym session down the leisure centre. We could meet up before school,' says Magda.

'What?'

'Stop it!' says Nadine. 'You two are going completely bananas. It's like something out of *The X-Files*. My two best friends have been taken over by crazed zombies. First Ellie gets this thing about being fat and gives up eating altogether – *Ellie*, the girl who once ate three Mars Bars on the trot! – and now Magda's saying she wants to get up at crack of dawn and go and work out in a gym. *Why?*'

I wonder if Magda's desperately envious about Nadine's modelling chance too. Then my brain starts working *properly*.

'This guy you met in the Soda Fountain – *he* doesn't happen to have an early morning gym session, does he?' I say.

'Aah!' says Nadine.

'No, Jamie doesn't,' says Magda. 'He's not into anything physical. Apart from sex. He can't keep his hands to himself. He's like an octopus. I'm not going out with *him* again.'

'No, but Jamie wasn't the one you really fancied. It was the dark dishy one. Mike?'

'*Mick*. Oooh, he is so gorgeous! He was round at Jamie's place the other day. He sat next to me on the sofa and OK, we weren't even touching, but it was like these electrical currents were going sizzle sizzle sizzle between him and me. I felt my hair was practically standing on end. I tried so hard with him and

65

I just know he's interested, but he's Jamie's best friend and he obviously doesn't want to cause trouble. He and Jamie are ever so close.'

'Maybe they're too close,' I say. 'Are you sure Mick isn't gay, Magda?'

'No, of course he's not gay! Look, OK, he did just happen to let slip that he works out at the Sun-risers club down the leisure centre—'

'Then I should think he *is* gay. Straight guys don't bother about their bodies half so much,' says Nadine, flexing her own arms. 'Hey, what do you think of my muscle definition? Do you think I ought to try to develop it?'

'Try developing your bust, darling,' says Magda, sticking out her own Wonderbra bosom.

'It's OK to be small. Lots of models are. And anyway, I could always go for a breast enhancement later,' says Nadine.

'Sounds like you're more in need of a *brain* enhancement,' I say sourly. 'And you, Magda. I'm not going to a sweaty old gym just so you can make out with this Mick.'

'OK OK, not the gym. Maybe it would be almost too obvious. Anyway, it costs a fortune. No, I thought we could go swimming? The pool opens at seven same as the gym. How about going just *once*? Ellie? Nadine? Then we could fetch up in the cafeteria for breakfast afterwards and surprise surprise, there's Mick. Hopefully. *Please!* I don't want to go on my own. I'll stand you both breakfast afterwards. They do super raspberry Danish pastries.'

'I'm on a diet,' I snap.

'Looks like your little ploy's not working, Magda. You can certainly count me out. I need my beauty sleep,' says Nadine.

'Ellie? Listen, I was reading this article about swimming, how it's the best exercise you can take because you're using every single muscle in your body, right – and if you go early in the morning, before you've eaten anything, it speeds up your metabolism so that whatever you eat after gets burnt up in double quick time. So you could eat up that raspberry Danish and not put on an ounce in weight.'

I know she's just shooting me a line. Yet maybe there's some truth in what she's saying. It sounds logical. Well, not the raspberry Danish bit, sadly. But if I could *really* kick-start my metabolism into superdrive every morning it might make a real difference.

'Yes, Ellie!' says Magda, seeing my face. 'I'll meet you outside the leisure centre at seven tomorrow morning, right?'

'Wrong,' I say. How can I go swimming and show off my great white whale body to everyone? And yet . . . half an hour's strong swimming would burn up so many calories . . .

'Just *once*, Ellie. Please. Pretty please.'

So I say I will. Just once.

I spend most of the evening peering at myself in my awful old swimming costume, convinced I cannot possibly expose myself in all my horrible wobbliness. Plus what should I do about all my hairy bits? I try shaving under my arms, snaffling Anna's razor, and cut myself, which smarts terribly.

I phone Magda to call the whole thing off. She tells me that swimming tautens all your muscles, and points out that even the biggest beefiest serious swimmer has a washboard stomach, tight bum and taut thighs. I miserably feel my flabby flesh as she speaks. I agree to go after all.

I feel like death getting up at quarter past six but the cold air revives me a little. I jog-shuffle most of the way to the leisure centre, deciding I might as well get in a little extra exercise on the way. I make good progress and get there at three minutes to seven, before the doors are even open. There's a little group of fitness freaks waiting, huddled into the hoods of their tracktops. Magda isn't here yet. There's no dark dishy hunk that could be Mick either. I stand in my school uniform, clutching my duffle bag, feeling horribly out of place. People will be wondering what on earth this squat blobby schoolgirl is doing at a fitness centre – *fat*ness centre, more like. There's an enviably thin girl in a green tracksuit staring at me right at this minute.

'Ellie?'

I stare back, startled. The thin girl is smiling. It's Zoë Patterson!

Zoë is famous at our school. She's a real brainbox. She should be in Year Ten but she's been put up a year to take all her GCSEs a year early. God knows how many she's doing – ten, eleven, maybe even twelve. I bet she gets As in all of them. Zoë wins her form prize every year. And the Art prize too.

That's how I know her. We both spend a lot of time in the art room doing all sorts of stuff, and when Mrs Lilley, the Art teacher, wanted a special mural to brighten the room up she asked Zoë and me to work on it together during our lunch hour.

We hardly spoke to each other at first. I thought it was because Zoë was older than me and might be a bit snobby, but then I realized she's actually even shyer than I am. So I got up the nerve to start talking to her and she soon got ever so friendly and funny. By the time we'd finished our mural (a crazy summer camp scene of all different creative women through time: we had Virginia Woolf with her skirts tucked in her drawers paddling in the stream, Jane Austen in an apron peeling potatoes, all the Brontë sisters with their sleeves rolled up sizzling sausages on the barbeque, Florence Nightingale pitching a tent, Billie Holliday picking flowers, Marilyn Monroe hanging out the washing, Frida Kahlo painting pictures on her welly boots) it seemed like we were firm friends.

But this school year Zoë hasn't been coming to the art room and whenever I've bumped into her in the corridors or the cloakroom we've just said hi and hurried on. I wondered if she'd gone off me or thought me too babyish or was maybe just too busy to be friendly when she was swotting for all those scary exams.

'Hi, Zoë. I never expected to see you here,' I say.

I assumed Zoë thought along the same lines as me when it came to sport.

'I come here every day,' says Zoë. 'Are you here to swim too?'

'Yes. I said I'd come with Magda. You know, my friend. The blond one. Though goodness knows when she's going to get here. I bet she's slept in.'

The doors open. I say I'd better wait for Magda so Zoë goes hurrying down to the changing room. She didn't used to be anywhere near as thin. She's got amazing cheekbones now. Her tracksuit bottom is all baggy. Zoë was never fat – not like me – but she used to be a bit pear-shaped with a biggish bum. Hey, maybe swimming really works!

I think I might start going every day too. Though not with Magda. She doesn't arrive until *twenty past.*

'Hi, Ellie. God, isn't it awful getting up this early,' she mumbles.

'You're not early, Magda, you're *late.*'

She's not taking any notice, peering all over the place as we go into the centre and pay for our swim.

'Have you seen anyone that looks like Mick, Ellie? You know, dark and truly dishy.'

'I don't know. Heaps of people have gone in. I didn't see anyone *that* fantastic – but we've got different taste when it comes to boys.'

'You're telling me,' says Magda. 'You've got Dan for a boyfriend.'

'He's not my *boy*friend,' I say.

'Well, what is he then?' says Magda.

'I don't know,' I say.

Dan was so keen on me it was embarrassing. We've fooled around a bit together in a totally chaste sort of way, but it's not been the Love Match of the Century. Or the year, month, week, day, minute. Scarcely Love Match of the *Second*. Though Dan's always insisted he loves me. I've never worked out whether he was totally serious. I'm even less sure now. He hasn't written to me recently. And he hasn't phoned me back since that time I phoned him and he was watching some stupid rugby match.

Maybe I need a new boyfriend.

Ha. Who would ever want to go out with me?

Plenty of boys want to go out with Magda. I can see why she was so late getting here. She's fully made up and her hair's freshly washed and styled. She wriggles into a new slinky scarlet lycra costume. It's so tight it must feel like wearing a full-size elastic band – but she looks incredible.

I turn my back to take off my clothes, embarrassed to strip off even in front of Magda. My hair sticks up in a giant bush, my face is all blotchy from the cold and yet in the sudden heat inside my glasses steam up so I can't see. It feels better when I take them off and shove them in my locker. If I can't see anyone clearly I can kid myself that maybe they can't see me.

I grope my way to the poolside and slide in as quickly as possible so that I'm hidden, up to my neck in sparkling turquoise water. It's beautifully warm, but Magda takes for ever to get in, standing on the side of the pool, dipping her toes in and squealing. It's obviously just to show herself off. It works. I swim two fast and furious laps and when I get back to the shallow end there are *five* boys surrounding Magda, laughing and jostling and offering her advice.

I swim off again. I'm trying not to mind. I'm not here to get off with boys anyway. I'm here to lose weight.

So I plough backwards and forwards, ten lengths breaststroke, ten lengths freestyle, ten lengths backstroke. Then repeat. Thank goodness I'm quite good at swimming so I don't look too stupid. Some of the boys are faster than me but I'm quicker than all the women – apart from Zoë.

We're about even-steven and find we can't help racing each other. First she steams ahead so I concentrate fiercely and push myself that little bit harder so that I'm gasping every time I take a breath. I draw closer, closer – and then I'm suddenly in front, and I whizz off even faster, but it's hard to keep it up. I'm slower the next lap, floating a little, and Zoë suddenly flashes past.

We carry on this mad competition and end up neck and neck, laughing at each other.

'We'd better get out now or we'll be late for school,' says Zoë.

'Right,' I say, scarcely able to draw breath.

Magda got out ages ago. She was barely *in*. She swam about ten measly lengths, keeping her head artificially high out of the water so that her hair wouldn't get messed up and then she was off back to the changing room to replenish her make-up.

She's hogging the mirror now, applying the finishing touches.

'Right, Ellie. See you in the café, OK?' she says. 'I don't want to miss Mick — *if* he's actually here.'

Zoë and I take a shower. We're very modest, looking away from each other as we soap ourselves under the streaming water but once we're towelling dry and stuffing damp bodies into underwear I take a quick glance at her when I've put my glasses on. I stare.

Zoë is thin. Not just slender. Not even skinny. Her ribs are sticking out of her skin, her pelvis juts alarmingly, her arms and legs look as if they're about to snap.

'Zoë!' I wonder if she's ill. I've never seen anyone this thin before. She looks *awful.*

'What?' she says, looking anxious.

'You've lost so much weight!'

'Not really. Not enough. Not yet,' says Zoë.

# Chapter Five

Turkeygirl

# Turkeygirl

I'm not stupid. I know Zoë's sick. She's obviously
anorexic. She's not thin and beautiful. She's thin and
sad. Thin and mad. She's starving herself. She looks
like a living skeleton. There's nothing desirable about
her gaunt body, her jutting bones, her beaky features.

I don't want to end up like Zoë.

I eat chicken and broccoli and baked potatoes for
supper. I even put butter inside my potatoes and
follow my first course with chocolate ice-cream
and extra chocolate sauce.

'Thank God,' says Dad. 'I was so sick of that stupid
diet. Have you seriously seen sense at last, Ellie?'

'You bet,' I say, running to the fridge and getting
out a second carton of chocolate ice-cream.

'Me too,' says Anna, getting her own bowl.

It feels so wonderful to eat my meal slowly,

76

savouring every mouthful. I feel full and warm and peaceful. I chat to Anna, I chat to Dad, I even chat to Eggs. I don't shut myself away in my bedroom after supper. I curl up on the sofa in the living room. Dad brings out his all-time favourite video, the one he loves us all to watch together when we're playing happy families. *The Wizard of Oz.*

I get a little tense watching Jady Garland at first. Is she too fat or is she just fine? She's thin compared to me. But when she steps out of her little grey house into the colour of Oz I step with her and stop worrying. I just sit back and enjoy the movie.

I take Eggs up to bed singing, 'Follow, follow, follow, follow, *follow* the purple stair cord', and we do a little Munchkin dance on the landing. His arms wind tight round my neck as I tuck him up in bed.

'I love you, Ellie,' he whispers.

'I love you too, Eggs,' I whisper back.

I wonder why I'm usually so mean to him. I don't feel like being mean to anyone now. I even give myself a grin in the mirror when I go into my bedroom. I have a tiny panic when I get undressed. My full tummy looks so big. I stand sideways and peer in the mirror to see just how much it's sticking out. But then I pull my nightie on quick and jump into bed. I think about the film. I click my bare heels in their invisible ruby slippers over and over again.

I try to cling to this new common sense next day at school. It's not easy. I feel so dumpy in my tight uniform. Nadine's skirt hangs so gracefully on her, in real folds. Mine is so taut it feels like my knees are tied

77

together. Nadine's sweater is so loose. Mine is strained over the jutting shelf of my chest. I stare at everyone. They all look much thinner than me. I can't seem to help myself. I even start staring at poor huge Alison Smith and wonder if we're of similar size.

I try to calm down in Art. Mrs Lilley says we can paint any kind of Christmas scene we fancy – and offers us a chocolate Father Christmas as a prize for the most amusing and original effort.

Magda does a glamorous male stripper wearing a few sprigs of holly in strategic places and a silly Santa beard. Nadine paints a fashion model fairy on top of a Christmas tree. I do an extremely anxious turkey, eyes bulging, wattle quivering, beak wedged open while a farmer shovels great scoopfuls of food down its throat. It's already so fat it can barely waddle. The turkey's tail is a great fuzz of feathers. It's starting to look uncomfortably like a self-portrait. Lithe little sparrows fly happily about the turkey's head, free as the wind. I can't seem to make it funny. It's sad.

'Oh dear, Ellie,' says Mrs Lilley. 'Have you joined an animal rights group?'

I don't win the chocolate Father Christmas. I don't know why I mind so much. It's not as if I'd neces-sarily eat the chocolate anyway, not at 529 terrible calories per 100 grammes. I have gloomily inspected every kind of chocolate bar for their calorific value and then shoved them back on the shelf quickly, as if even handling them could make you fat.

Mrs Lilley is looking a little tubby lately, come to think of it. She's always been quite skinny but now she's getting a bit of a tummy and her waist is thicker too. Yet she looks OK in her denim shirt and waistcoat and long black skirt. She's wearing a big chunk of dark amber on a long black cord round her neck. Her eyes glow the same colour. She's looking great even though she's definitely put on a good half stone, maybe more, during this term. She doesn't seem to care. She looks really happy.

I think of pale sick skinny Zoë. I don't really wish I looked like her, do I? Maybe I could go in for the Mrs Lilley look, plumpish but still pretty in lovely loose clothes. Artistic.

I *wish* I'd won the chocolate Father Christmas.

Mrs Lilley calls me over to her desk at the end of the lesson.

'I'm sorry you didn't get the prize, Ellie,' she says.

'That's OK.'

'You know I think you're really gifted at Art, don't you?'

'Thank you.' I know I'm going red.

'I do hope I can come back long before you do your Art GCSE.'

'Come back?'

'I'm leaving at the end of this term.'

'Oh Mrs Lilley, *why*?'

She smiles at me.

'I thought you'd guessed! I saw you staring at my tummy today.' She pats it gently. 'I'm going to have a baby.'

'Ooh!'

'Yes, I didn't show for a while, but now I'm fast

approaching the waddling stage. I feel like your poor Christmas turkey.'

I feel like bursting into tears.

'Cheer up, Ellie. Maybe you can come and see me sometime after I've had the baby.'

'Mm, maybe. Well. Congratulations.'

I have to rush away. Mrs Lilley isn't fat. She is pregnant. My role model for a reasonable figure – *still* thinner than me – is probably six months pregnant.

Oh, God.

Anna is preparing a huge spag bol when I get home from school.

'I can't eat *that*!' I say, appalled.

I eat half a small tub of cottage cheese garnished with chopped cucumber and carrots. It looks and tastes disgusting, as if someone else has already eaten it and thrown it up. The smell of spaghetti bolognese makes me feel faint but I manage to hold out. Somehow. If only I could seal my lips with Superglue, then I'd feel really safe.

I even dream about it at night and wake up sucking my own hand. I curl up tight and clasp myself. I mustn't creep down to the kitchen and raid the fridge. I daren't have another stuff-my-face session because Anna might hear if I make myself sick.

I'm scared of getting really bulimic. I read an article in Nadine's *Spicy* magazine (she's its most avid reader now) and it says if you keep throwing up the acid rots your teeth. This famous model went through a six-month spell of being sick to keep in trim for her fashion work and now she's had to have a full set of false teeth fitted.

'Thank goodness I'm naturally slim,' Nadine says smugly, reading over my shoulder.

I make sick noises myself. Nadine isn't half getting on my nerves at the moment. I ask her privately what she thinks of Zoë, pointing her out in Assembly.

'How do you mean?'

'Well, don't you think she's sort of weird now?' I don't want to prompt Nadine in any way, I want her honest opinion.

'Zoë's *always* been weird. She's such a swot. All those prizes every year. Why doesn't she get a life?' Nadine says heartlessly.

'Yes, but don't you think she *looks* weird now,' I say. 'Haven't you noticed she's got a lot thinner?'

Nadine glances at Zoë again. She's bunched up in her baggy school uniform. Her skirt's much longer than anyone else's and she's wearing very thick woolly tights. There isn't really much of her on show.

'I suppose she's got a bit skinny, yeah,' says Nadine, as if it's no big deal.

Maybe it isn't. Maybe Zoë is a perfect size now. After all, she really did have a biggish bum before. But now she's worked as hard as always and she's won the slimming stakes too.

I struggle to remember exactly what she looks like without her clothes. Different sized Zoës dance in my head like reflections in a crazy mirror show. I can't work out which is the right one. I need to know.

'Coming swimming tomorrow, Magda?' I say.

81

'There's not much point. Mick wasn't there, was he?' says Magda.

'Still, look at all those other boys who started chatting you up.'

'They were OK, I suppose. Larry, the fair one, asked me out, as a matter of fact. I said I might meet up with him this weekend.'

'*When*?' says Nadine. 'Oh, Mags, you've got to help me with my hair and my make-up and everything. It's the *Spicy* heat!'

'You still like Mick best, don't you?' I persist. 'Come swimming tomorrow. You come too, Nadine – you want to be in good shape for Saturday.'

'Yes, but I don't want my hair all mucked up with chlorine,' says Nadine. 'And I'm trying to get eight hours sleep every night this week. I don't want bags under my eyes. I can't get up ultra-early.'

Magda can't get up ultra-early either. She keeps me hanging around outside the pool for ages. Zoë arrives when I do, jogging along the path, her face screwed up with concentration. She carries on jogging on the spot while she's in the queue, as if her trainers are fitted with springs.

'How can you be so energetic so early in the morning, Zoë?' I say.

'I've been up since five,' says Zoë, panting a little. '*What?*'

'I have to, to get everything done. I do some stretching and some sit-ups, and then an hour's studying. I'm desperate to get my own exercise bike at home and then I could set up my books so I could read *and* work out. It's mad, my mum and dad are forking out a fortune to spend Christmas in this posh hotel in Portugal and I've begged them to let me stay at home and with the money they save on my fare they could buy me the bike, but they won't *listen.*' Zoë talks faster than she used to, as if her thoughts have speeded up. 'My dad's just doing this to spite me. He's admitted it. He wants to fatten me up. He's *sick.*'

I wish I had the courage to contradict her. *She's* the one who's sick, only she can't see it. Or *is* she? She's extremely fit so she must be healthy. She's top of her class. Best at everything. Especially Art.

'Do you still paint, Zoë?'

'Well, just my GCSE work.'

'You don't do any art just for fun? You know, like when we did that mural together in the art room?'

Zoë shakes her head, looking pitying.

'I don't really have time for that sort of stuff nowadays,' she says, as if I'm a toddler wondering why she won't do finger-painting with me.

She disappears inside the pool. I hang around waiting for Magda. I see a tall dark hunky guy in a very stylish black sweatsuit go through to the Gym. I wonder if he's Mick? I can't really *ask*. The bunch of boys who were all over Magda the other day are here too. The fair one asks me where my friend is.

'She's coming,' I say.

One of them mutters and they all snigger.

I blush, hating them. I'm not going to stand about

any longer. Why should I always wait hours for Magda? And I *must* see Zoë.

I push past the boys and go through to the changing rooms. Zoë is already undressed, bending over her bag looking for her goggles. Her back is alarmingly ridged with her vertebrae. It looks as if her spine could snap straight through her skin. She hasn't got any flesh anywhere. I can see all the cords and tendons in her legs as she stretches. She straightens up and I see there's a gap between her thighs now so that she looks bow-legged. When she reaches up to put on her goggles her breasts are two little puckers on her rib cage, nothing more. There are great ugly grooves around her throat and collarbone. Her face is so shrunken in on itself you can see the shape of her skull. She is seriously starving herself to death.

But when she shivers through the shower, raising her fragile arms, her tummy totally flat in her skintight lycra costume, I still feel a stab of envy. I *must* lose weight. I want to be thin. All right, not as thin as Zoë. Not sick. But she's shown me you *can* change yourself. Last year Zoë might have been nearly my size. Now she's much thinner than Magda, thinner than Nadine, thinner than anyone I've ever seen, apart from those poor starving children you see on the news on television.

I'm going to be thin too. It's simple. I just won't eat. And yet all the time I'm thrashing up and down the pool I think Danish Pastry – golden, succulent, oozing jam. Magda turns up at last, in her strawberry swimsuit and matching red waterproof lipstick. She smiles her oh-so-jammy smile and all the boys hurtle down to her end of the pool and surround her.

When I can get her on her own for half a second I tell her that a guy exactly her description of Mick is busy pumping iron in the gym. Magda's own muscles clench excitedly.

'Great! Well, we'll get out soon, right, and go for breakfast.'

'There's no point coming here and swimming like crazy, just to make myself even fatter,' I say.

'You're not fat,' Magda says automatically. Then she glances down at me as I hunch under the turquoise water. 'And you're getting thinner now anyway.'

'What? Really? How much thinner? Or are you just saying it to get round me?'

'Ellie, you're paranoid. *Yes*, you're thinner. How much weight have you lost?'

'Only about five pounds so far.'

'Well, there you go. You look five pounds thinner. That's heaps. So you can come and have a yummy Danish pastry with me and help me go Mickspotting.'

'There! I *knew* you were just saying it.'

'It's true. Look, you're going to go seriously anorexic if you're not careful. You'll end up a bag of bones like that poor sad Zoë.'

'You think Zoë's almost too thin then?' I ask eagerly.

Magda stares at me.

'Wake *up*, Ellie. She looks terrible. I'm amazed they don't cart her straight off to hospital. I don't know how her parents can let her get like that.'

'Her dad's taking her away at Christmas to feed her up.'

'He'll have to give her twenty meals a day then – she's like a skeleton.' Magda drops her voice as Zoë zips to our end of the pool and hauls herself up the steps.

I stare at her stick limbs. She's shivering, her hands pale purple with the cold. I watch the papery skin across her ribs as she gasps for breath. I know Magda is right – and yet I jog to school with Zoë rather than have breakfast in the café with Magda.

Zoë might be seriously ill but she's far fitter than me. I'm staggering in agony by the time I get to school. Mrs Henderson finds me in a state of collapse on the cloakroom floor.

'Ellie? What is it?'

'I'm . . . just . . . out of . . . breath.'

'I thought you were having an asthma attack. Have you been *running*? And you're not even late for school!'

'I've run all the way from the leisure centre,' I gasp.

'My goodness. I think *I* need to sit down. Eleanor Allard on a fitness kick!'

'I've actually never felt *less* fit in my life,' I say, clutching my chest. 'I think I'm having a heart attack.'

'Maybe you need to come to my lunchtime aerobic session,' says Mrs Henderson.

'OK, maybe I will,' I say.

It'll burn off two or three hundred calories – *and* stop me craving lunch. It's a special lunch today, the cook's traditional Christmas dinner treat for the end of term. Turkey, one chipolata sausage, two roast potatoes, a dollop of mash and garden peas, and then mincemeat tart with a blob of artificial cream. We're talking mega-calories per trayful.

I can't risk setting foot inside the canteen. I go to the aerobic session. It's hell. Total burning hellfire.

I feel such a fool amongst all the seriously-fit muscle-girls leaping about in their luminous lycra. I stand behind Zoë, who is bunched up in a huge T-shirt and tracksuit bottoms. She looks hopelessly weak and weedy, but she's fighting fit. She never misses a beat, her lips a tight line of effort.

I get so hot I can't see out my glasses and the spring goes out of my hair. I've got such a stitch I have to fight not to double up. I still try to swing my arms and stamp my legs but they've turned to jelly.

'Take two minutes' break, Ellie,' Mrs Henderson calls.

I crash to the floor. Gasp gasp gasp. But I'm not going to lose any weight lying here going wibble-wobble. I drag myself up and get going again. I last to the end of the session . . . just.

I've got to take a shower, obviously, but I seriously hate the school showers because there aren't any curtains at all. I hunch in a corner, trying to keep my back to everyone, taking envious peeks at all the taut thighs and flat tummies surrounding me.

Zoë avoids this ordeal. She runs off in her sweaty T-shirt clutching a sponge bag, obviously going to have a little wash in the toilets.

I shove my school uniform over my sticky pink blancmange body as quickly as possible. Mrs Henderson catches hold of me.

'Can I have a word, Ellie? Come in my changing room.'

Oh, God. The only times I've been invited into her inner sanctum it's to get severely told off for pretending to have a permanent heavy period to get me out of games. She's surely not going to tell me off for volunteering for *extra* games?

'So, Ellie, what's going on? First it's swimming, then running, now aerobics. Why?'

'You told me to come along this lunchtime.'

'I was joking – though it was certainly a pleasant surprise when you turned up. But I just wonder what you're playing at, Ellie.'

'I told you. I'm trying to get fit. I thought you'd be thrilled to bits, Mrs Henderson. You're always nagging at me to take more exercise. So I am.'

'Do you want to get fit, Ellie – or thin?'

'What?'

'I'm not stupid. I know why poor Zoë comes to aerobics. I'm very worried about her. I've tried talking to her umpteen times – and her parents. She's obviously severely anorexic. But I want to talk about you, Ellie, not Zoë.'

'You can hardly call me anorexic, Mrs Henderson,' I say, looking down at my body with loathing. 'I'm fat.'

'You've lost weight recently.'

'Only a few pounds, hardly anything.'

'You've done very well. But you mustn't lose weight too rapidly. You girls go on all these crazy diets but all you really have to do is cut down on all the sweets and chocolate and crisps and eat *sensibly*. Lots of fresh fruit, vegetables, fish, chicken, pasta. You *are* eating a reasonably balanced diet, aren't you, Ellie?'

'*Yes*, Mrs Henderson.'

One apple. Two sticks of celery. Half a tub of cottage cheese. One Ryvita. Fruit, veg, protein, carbohydrate. Brilliantly balanced.

'Because you're a perfectly healthy normal ordinary size, Ellie.'

'Ordinary – for an elephant.'

'I *mean* it. What's brought all this on, hmm?' Mrs Henderson looks at me. 'It wouldn't have anything to do with Nadine suddenly acting as if she's the second Kate Moss?'

'*No!*' I say, perhaps a little too fiercely.

'Do *you* want to be a fashion model, Ellie?' says Mrs Henderson.

'Me?' I say, snorting at the idea.

How could I ever get to be a model? OK, I could staple my lips together for good and starve myself slim. But what could I do with my mane of frizzy hair, my little owl glasses, my dumpy five foot two physique?

Mrs Henderson misunderstands the true meaning of my snort.

'Ah! At least you haven't dieted away your basic common sense, Ellie. You seem to share my feelings

89

about fashion models and their ludicrous strutting and vacant posing. Why can't girls ache to be scientists or surgeons?'

'Count me out, Mrs Henderson. I come nearly bottom in Science – and I can't stand the sight of blood so I doubt I'd make a very good surgeon either.'

'*You're* going to be an artist,' says Mrs Henderson.

I blink at her, going red.

'What do you mean?' I stammer. I didn't have a clue Mrs Henderson knew I even *like* Art.

'We teachers do talk amongst ourselves, you know. It sounds as if you're Mrs Lilley's pet pupil.'

'Yes, but she's leaving.'

'Then you'll doubtless be the new art teacher's pet pupil too,' says Mrs Henderson.

'She'll probably think I can't draw for toffee,' I say.

Stupid word. I think of soft gooey buttery brown toffee and my mouth drips with saliva. Do I like toffee best – or fudge? No, nougat, the sort with the cherries. I open my lips and imagine chewing a huge sticky slab of nougat . . .

'Ellie? Are you listening to me?' says Mrs Henderson.

'Yes, of course,' I say, swallowing my imaginary sweets. 'Don't worry, Mrs Henderson. I swear I don't want to be a model. I couldn't care less about Nadine and her big chance. Honestly.'

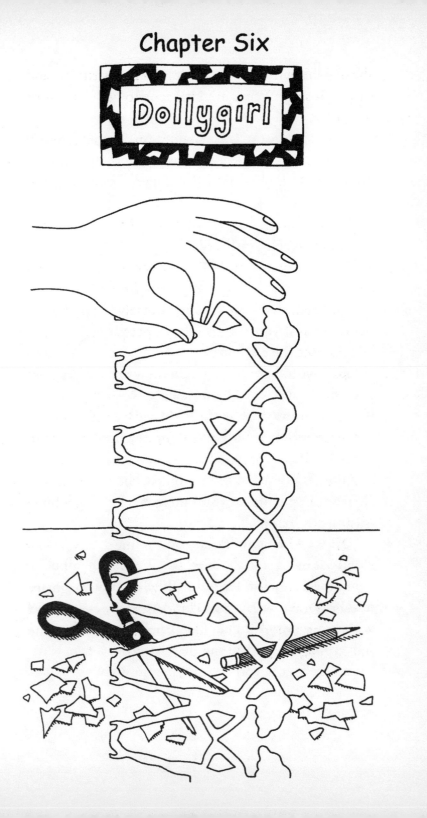

# Chapter Six

# Dollygirl

I was going to keep right out of it on Saturday. Magda had promised to go with Nadine. It was all settled. But then Mick *un*settled everything. Magda shared her Danish pastry with him at the leisure centre – and now has him eating out of her hand.

'He's asked me to go to this football match on Saturday,' she says.

'Oh wow! Date of the century,' I say.

Magda is eating a Mars bar. She's been nibbling along the top with her little white teeth like a chipmunk, and now she's licking the exposed caramel with her pointy tongue. The smell of the chocolate is overpowering. I want to snatch it from her so badly I can barely concentrate on what she's saying.

Nadine is looking at her with laser beam eyes.

'Not *this* Saturday?'

'Mm.'

'But you can't. You're going to make me up.'

'Yes, yes, well, I can still do that, can't I? The match is in the afternoon, *right*?'

'But you're coming *with* me.'

'Well . . . you don't really need me there, do you?'

'We're supposed to go with someone. It *says*. Relative or friend.'

'They probably mean an adult friend, as a chaperone. So you'd really better go with your mum.'

'I'm not going with my *mother*. Are you crazy? What sort of an idiot would I look, trotting along with her. I haven't even told her about it. You know what she's like. Dear goodness, she'd get me to perm my hair in ringlets and put me in a frilly frock!'

'OK, OK, point made. Go with Ellie.'

'What?' I say, snapping to attention. 'No!'

'But I can't go on my own! Magda, you can't stand me up to watch a lousy football match!'

'Mick's *playing*, Nadine. He said I'd bring him luck. I *can't* stand him up. We're going out after too. It's my big chance with him, I just know it is.'

'It's *my* big chance on Saturday. I can't believe you could be so selfish,' says Nadine, nearly in tears. 'You're letting me down just for some stupid boy. That's just typical of you, Magda.' She turns to me. 'Ellie?'

'No! I'm not going with you, Nadine. I can't. I won't.'

But she keeps going on and on at me. So on Saturday morning I go with her to Magda's. Magda

93

is already carefully got up in her version of football watching gear: scarlet sweater that clings to every curve, label-to-die-for jeans and high-heeled boots, with her beautiful fur jacket to keep her cosy.

'OK, Nadine, let's get cracking,' she says, rolling up the sleeves of her sweater.

'I don't want anything too bright,' Nadine says anxiously.

'Just leave it to me, OK?'

'I mean, I can see that my usual look isn't quite right—'

'Your chalk-white just-stepped-out-your-coffin look? Yeah, you'd frighten them to death.'

'But I can't be too colourful. Look at the way all these girls look in the magazine.' Nadine stabs her finger at various models in *Spicy* magazine. 'They look . . . natural.'

'Right. Natural,' says Magda, scraping Nadine's hair back.

'You can *do* natural, can't you, Magda?' says Nadine.

'I won't do anything at all if you carry on. Now lie back and shut up.'

It takes Magda nearly an hour to get Nadine looking natural enough. I can't help being riveted. It's so weird seeing her blossom beneath Magda's deft fingers.

'There!' she says at last, holding the mirror up for Nadine. 'You like?'

'Well . . . I don't know. I look ever so pink and girly. Can't we rub off some of the blusher?'

94

'Don't you dare touch it! It's perfect. Now, your hair.'

'Yes. What am I going to *do* about it?' says Nadine, running her fingers through it despairingly.

'What's the matter with it?' I say. It looks lovely. It always does. It's a long black shiny waterfall, glinting almost blue when it catches the light.

I've always loved Nadine's hair and wished that my own hair could somehow be shocked out of its corkscrew curls. When we were little girls I'd brush Nadine's glossy long hair until it crackled. When we slept at each other's houses I'd cuddle up close to Nadine and pretend that the shiny dark hair on the pillow touching my shoulder really belonged to me.

I remember *that* – and yet I *don't* remember longing for Nadine's body to set off her long glossy hair. I knew that I was quite a fat little girl and Nadine a thin one – but it didn't really bother me then.

It's really weird – the me *then* won't match up with the me *now*. I wish I could still be the old Ellie. It's so hard being this new one. It's such a battle all the time. I feel so sick now because I didn't dare have anything for breakfast and I don't know what I'm going to do about tea this evening because we always have takeaways on Saturdays and they always smell so good and yet they're all hundreds and hundreds and hundreds of calories, flakey white fish in golden crunchy batter with mounds of salty savoury chips, or a great Catherine wheel of pizza sizzling with cheese, or tangy tandoori chicken, ruby red and hot, with pearly rice to fill my empty aching stomach . . .

'Ellie!' says Magda, busy parting Nadine's hair. 'Is that your stomach rumbling?'

'I can't help it,' I say, going red.

'What about a little plaity bit on top?' says Magda.

'I was wondering about lots of little plaits,' says Nadine, holding her head on one side and fiddling with wisps of her hair.

'Plaits!' I say. 'Come on. How childish can you get.'

'Not childish. Cute,' says Magda, starting to plait.

'Look at this girl – *she's* got little plaits,' says Nadine, stabbing her finger at *Spicy* magazine. 'Yeah, plaits, please, Mags.'

The plaiting process takes for ever. I yawn and sigh and fiddle and clench my stomach to shut it up.

'This is s-o-o-o-o boring,' I moan. 'What are you going to wear anyway, Nadine?'

'What I've got on!' says Nadine.

I stare at her. I thought she was wearing dreary old things to save her posh outfit getting mucked up. Nadine usually wears amazing clothes, black velvet, black lace, black leather. Now today of all days she's got on just an ordinary pair of blue jeans and a skimpy little pink T-shirt.

'Why aren't you wearing anything black? You don't look like you,' I say.

'That's the whole point. I want to look like a model,' says Nadine.

'But shouldn't you dress up a bit?' I ask.

'Take no notice of Ellie, she hasn't got a clue,' says Magda, sighing.

'This is the sort of stuff models wear when they go on shoots,' says Nadine. 'You dress down, see. Though these jeans are French and cost a fortune. My mum's going to do her nut when she finds out I've drawn out some of my building society money.'

'Yeah, but think of the fortune you might be earning soon, Nadine,' says Magda. 'And the minute you've made it, you're to start introducing me to all the right people, OK? The rounded voluptuous look is very in too. They don't just want stringbeans like you.'

'Dream on,' I say sourly.

What if Nadine *does* make it as a model? She looks so different now. I stare at her and it suddenly all seems real. She looks just like all the models in *Spicy* magazine. She'll win this heat. She'll go through to the final. She'll get to be the *Spicy* cover girl. She'll be photographed with a pretty little pout for all the magazines, she'll prance up and down the catwalks, she'll jet across the world on special fashion shoots . . . and I'll stay put, still at school, Nadine's sad fat friend.

I feel as if this title is tattooed to my forehead as I go up to London with Nadine. I have to go with her because she *is* my friend. I've put almost as much thought into my appearance as Nadine has with hers. I've left my hair an untamed tangle, my face is belligerently bare, I'm wearing a huge checked shirt and black trousers and boots, and I'm carrying my sketch book to try to show every single person at the *Spicy* place that *I* don't want to be a model, *I* couldn't care less about my appearance, I'm serious-minded,

I'm *creative* . . . OK, OK, I'm talking crap, I know. And *they* know when we get to the special studio *Spicy* magazine has taken over for the day.

It is crowded out with a galaxy of gorgeous girls, thin as pins.

'Oh, God, look at them,' Nadine says. She shivers. 'They all look like real fashion models already.'

'Well, so do you,' I say.

'Oh Ellie,' says Nadine, and she squeezes my hand. She's clammy-cold, clinging tight like we're little kids in Primary One on our first day at school.

'I wonder what we're going to have to do?' she says. 'If I have to stand up in front of all these girls I'm going to die. They all look so cool, as if they do this kind of thing every day.'

They do too. They're all standing around in little groups, some chatting, some smiling, some staring, looking everyone up and down, looking at Nadine, looking at me, raising their perfectly plucked eyebrows as if to say: Dear God, what is that squat ugly fat girl doing here?

I try to stare back. My face is burning.

'I'm desperate for a wee, Ellie. Where's the Ladies?' Nadine asks.

It's even worse inside the crowded Ladies room. Girls crowd the mirror, applying glimmer eyeshadow and sparkle blusher and lip gloss so that their perfect oval faces are positively luminous in the strobe lighting. They tease their hair and hitch up their tiny jeans and smooth their weeny T-shirts with long manicured nails.

'Help, look at *my* nails,' Nadine wails. She clenches her fists to hide her little bitten stubs. 'Oh God, this is a waste of time, Ellie. Why did I ever open my big mouth to everyone at school? I don't stand a chance. I must be mad.'

'Well, we don't have to stay. We can just push off home again.'

Nadine looks at me like *I'm* mad. 'I can't give up now!'

'OK. Well. The very best of luck, Naddie,' I say, and I give her a quick hug.

'I'm so scared,' she whispers in my ear, hugging me back.

But she's fine when it comes to the crunch. All us friends and relatives are told to sit at the back, minding the coats and bags, knowing our place in the dark. All the model girl contenders are invited to come forward into the spotlit area. A bright bossy woman in black tells everyone what to do. She says she thinks everyone looks great and that they could *all* be a super *Spicy* cover girl. She wishes everyone luck. Then she gets them to do these funny warm-up exercises. Some of the girls blush and bump into each other first, losing their cool – but others leap into action, teeth gleaming, determined to show themselves off to their best advantage.

I'd planned to make sketches but instead I just gawp. Enviously. I stare at their long lithe limbs and their beautiful willowy bodies until my eyes water.

The bossy lady shows them how to walk like a model now. They all have to prance forwards, hips swinging, heads held high. Nadine catches my eye and goes a bit giggly, but then she puts her chin up and strides out, her mouth parted in a perfect little smile. I put my thumbs up, trying to spur her on. She's doing well. Maybe she's not quite as swishy and sophisticated as some of the others but perhaps that's good. They want someone with potential, not someone already polished. Nadine looks fresh and sweet. The bossy lady is looking in her direction.

Now it's standing still and posing time. They take group shots of all the girls smiling at the camera, then looking up, sideways on, head tilted. They keep calling out to the girls. Look sassy, look sad, look happy – call that happy, come *on*, it's happy-happy-happy time. My own mouth puckers in a silly little grin as all the girls bare their teeth. Some of the friends and relations really let rip. One terrible mum keeps shouting 'Go for it, Hayley! Big smile now. Look like you're enjoying it. You look a million dollars, darling!'

It's easy working out which one is Hayley. She's the girl who's purple with embarrassment, looking like she wants to kill her mother.

There's a coffee break and then suddenly it's the real thing. The girls are called out one by one in alphabetical order. They are videoed as they walk right round in a big circle and then stand in the spot-light in the centre and pose while a stills photographer flashes away. Then each girl has to go to the mike and say who she is and add a sentence or two about herself.

Hayley's surname is Acton, so she gets to go first. She makes a muck-up of it, tripping over her own feet as she walks in a circle, blinking like a trapped rabbit while she's photographed. She stammers her name into the mike and then there's a long silence while everyone closes their eyes and prays. Eventually she whispers 'I don't know what to say.'

My shirt is sticking to me with embarrassment. The poor girl. Oh God, I'm not going to be able to stand it if Nadine makes a fool of herself too. Hayley's mother can't stand it either. She's rushed up to the bossy woman, insisting that it's not fair her Hayley had to go first, she didn't know what she was doing, all the others would have someone to copy (though who would wish to copy poor Hayley?). The bossy woman is kind and says Hayley can wait if she wants and have one more go right at the end. Hayley's mother is thrilled. Hayley isn't. She's walking right out of the studio.

'Hayley! Hayley, come back! Don't go, sweet-heart! You can have another go, darling,' Mum yells, rushing after her.

I am glad I'm not Hayley, even though she's much thinner than me. The girl who gets to go next is almost as nervous, practically running round the circle. She forgets about posing for her photos and is in the middle of announcing herself when the photographer starts flashing so she stops and blinks and gawps. This is awful, total public torture. I'm starting to feel almost sorry for them.

Almost. The next girl is blond and tall, very

pretty, very skinny. She doesn't lose it like the other two. She walks proudly all around, swinging her tiny hips, and then she stands and smiles, head back a little, eyes shining, turning this way and that as the photographer clicks. She says softly and sexily into the mike 'Hi, I'm Annabel. I'm fifteen and I like acting and singing and skiing – and reading *Spicy* magazine.' She smiles cheekily and then saunters off. Little Ms Perfect.

I catch Nadine's eye from across the room and mime being sick. I *feel* sick when it's Nadine's turn. My own legs wobble as she strides out. My own mouth aches as she smiles bravely.

Nadine walks in a perfect circle, slowly, gracefully, with a little bouncy twirl as she steps into the spotlight. She smiles at the guy with the camera and he waves his fingers at her. She poses brilliantly, turning this way and that. All those hours staring at herself in her bedroom mirror have paid off at last. She seems entirely at her ease. She doesn't blink when the camera flashes right in her face. She smiles at the lens. Then she reaches for the mike.

'Hello, I'm Nadine,' she says. 'I'm nearly fourteen. It feels weird to be standing here looking so girly. I usually have a white face and black clothes. My best friend Ellie calls me a vampire. But it's OK, I actually feel faint at the sight of blood.' She bares her teeth in a jokey way and everyone laughs and claps.

Fancy Nadine mentioning me! She's so clever to say all that stuff so that people like her and remember her.

'Great, Nadine. Well done,' I whisper as she comes

over to join me. I give her a hug. 'Hey, you're *shaking*.'

'It was so scary standing there with everyone staring,' she whispers. 'I didn't make a complete idiot of myself, did I?'

'No, you were great. Honestly. Heaps and heaps better than the others – even that awful Annabel.'

'Do you think I should have said I read *Spicy* magazine too?'

'No, it sounded far too sucky. What you said was brilliant. I can't believe you could do it all so well. I couldn't have acted like that in a million years.'

I couldn't – even if I was as thin and striking as Nadine. She's sitting cross-legged like a little girl, her neck bent so that her hair falls forward, the weeny plaits looking cute. Her jeans are almost baggy on her she's so skinny. Her tiny T-shirt is taut against her body. She doesn't have even one little roll of fat sitting hunched up like that. Her elbows stick out, delicately pointed, emphasizing the skinniness of her arms.

It's so *unfair*. Nadine eats like a horse. On cue she fumbles in her jacket pocket and finds a Twix bar. She offers me a chocolate stick.

'I'm on a *diet*.'

'Oh. Right. Sorry,' she says, munching. 'Yum. I'm starving – I was too het up to eat any breakfast.'

I didn't have breakfast either. Or any supper last night. It's easier to skip a meal altogether rather than discipline myself to nibble just a tiny amount. Once my mouth starts chomping I can't stop it. I

103

breathe in the rich chocolatey smell wistfully.

'Don't look at me like that, Ellie. You make me feel bad,' says Nadine, gobbling the last little bit. 'Still, you've done ever so well. I never thought you'd keep it up like this. You've lost quite a bit of weight now.'

'No, I haven't.'

'You *have*. Look at your tum!' Nadine reaches across and pats my tummy.

I try to suck it in, hating even Nadine to feel how huge it is.

'It's all gone. Practically flat,' says Nadine.

'I wish,' I say sourly.

We sit through endless hours while each girl has her go. I stare at their stomachs, all much much flatter than mine. I cuddle into my check shirt and under cover of its enveloping material I pinch my waist viciously, wishing I could tear pieces off with my fingertips.

Some of the girls are so nervous they muck it up like Hayley. Some of the girls are so gorgeous they prance professionally like Annabel.

'Only three girls get chosen from each area,' Nadine whispers. 'I haven't got a chance.'

'Yes you have! Wait and see. You'll walk it. You're heaps more attractive than any of the others.'

'Not that Annabel.'

'*Especially* that Annabel.'

But when they announce the winners Annabel is the first to be chosen. Then another blonde, an Annabel clone.

Nadine tenses beside me, praying so hard I can

almost see a please–please–please speech bubble above her head. I squeeze her hand. The third girl is announced. There's one squeal of triumph – and dozens of sighs all round the room. It isn't Nadine. It's a redhead with long white limbs and big green eyes, a striking girl, but she can't hold a candle to Nadine.

'It's not *fair*!' I wail.

Nadine says nothing. She looks totally stunned.

'So – is that it?' she says. She swallows hard. She's trying not to burst into tears.

Some girls are already crying, and another mother from hell is remonstrating with the bossy lady, demanding to know why her daughter wasn't picked.

'All you girls did splendidly. You look model-girl marvellous,' says the bossy lady into the mike. 'I just wish it were possible to pick you all. Thanks so much for taking part. Have a safe journey home – and please pick up a complimentary copy of *Spicy* magazine on your way out.'

It's the last thing most of the girls want to look at now.

'Never mind, Nad. It's obviously a total lottery. You still look terrific.'

Nadine shakes her head, her face contorted.

'I look idiotic,' she says, unravelling her cute plaits, tugging so hard it's a wonder her hair doesn't come out in handfuls. 'Come on, let's get out of here, Ellie.' She starts pushing her way through the crowd, her lips pressed tight together, a vein standing out on her pale forehead.

'Hey, hang on! You! The dark girl!'

Nadine whips round, sudden hope flashing across her face – but it's just the photographer.

'Bad luck. I really thought you were in with a chance when I spotted you at that shopping centre.'

Nadine shrugs bravely. 'I just came along for a laugh,' she lies.

'I still think you've got a hell of a lot of potential. I don't know what you've done with yourself today though. You don't stand out from the others. I didn't even recognize you at first. You should have stayed with the white face and the dramatic sweep of hair.'

'Oh!' says Nadine, stricken.

'Never mind. You could really make it as a model, you know. You should get yourself a decent port-folio. Look, here's my card. Give me a buzz and I'll take the photos for you at my studio. I'll have to charge, of course, but as you're a half-pint I'll do you for half price.'

'Oh, right! Great!' Nadine burbles.

I seize her wrist and drag her away.

'Hang on, Ellie! Oh wow! Look, he gave me his card. And he says he'll photograph me half-price.'

'And probably half-*clothed*. For God's sake, Nadine, get real. It's the oldest con trick in the world. That's just such a seriously sleazy offer, can't you see that?'

'No, it's not. He's *nice*. He says I've got real poten-tial. He's a professional photographer so he ought to know.'

'Yes, I bet he gave his card to half the girls here today.'

'Well, maybe you're just being bitchy because he didn't give his card to *you*,' Nadine snaps. 'Fat chance of that!'

She stops. I stop. We both stand still in the street outside the studio. Nadine's words buzz in the air, sharp as stings.

'Thanks,' I say weakly.

'Oh Ellie. I didn't mean it to sound like that.'

'Yes, you did,' I say. 'Look, I came today when I didn't want to, I tried to be ever so helpful and supportive, I've sat for hours and hours and *hours* watching all you lot, I've tried to stop you minding too much when you didn't get chosen – and when that cheesy photographer hits on you I try to make you see this is a seriously dodgy proposition – because I'm your *friend*, Nadine. Not because I'm a fat jealous bitch. I'm sorry you feel that way.' I turn on my heel and march off. Nadine follows me, tucking her hand in my arm, telling me she's really sorry.

'Of course you're not a bitch, Ellie. *I'm* a bitch for saying it. Oh come on, don't go all moody on me. I'm the one who should be cast down with gloom because I didn't get chosen.'

I let her carry on as long as possible, rather enjoying it. We pass lots of would-be model girls, all of them letting off steam. Several are quarrelling just like us. One girl is being dragged along towards us by her mother.

'It's not just that you've let *me* down so badly. You've let yourself down too,' the mother shrieks. 'Now we're going back to the studio and you're going to ask them to give you another chance.'

Oh God. It's Hayley. Her mum's managed to drag her all the way back – though it's too late now.

'Never mind poor you and poor me. Poor Hayley,' I say.

'Poor poor Hayley,' says Nadine. 'Ellie – are you still in a huff?'

'Sure, I'm as huffy as hell,' I say, putting my arm round her.

It's a pain maintaining my self-righteous pose. I'm ready to make friends too. On the train going home we see a whole load of boys playing footie and we wonder if Magda's Mick is one of them. We strain our eyes but don't spot her blond head and fur jacket on the sidelines.

'I wonder where they'll go after? Do you think he'll take her out clubbing?' I ask.

'No, he'll be too knackered after playing football. A meal, is my bet. Hey, shall *we* go out for a meal, Ellie? My treat, because you've been a real pal today.'

'Not a meal. My diet.'

'Oh, Ellie. Look, we could go for a pizza and you could just have a weeny slice and some salad.'

'*No*, Nadine.'

'You're still mad at me.'

'No, I'm not. Though I don't exactly relish being called a fat bitch.'

'I didn't! *You* said that.'

'But you implied it.'

'No I didn't. Listen, if you don't mind my saying so, Ellie, you're getting positively paranoid.'

'So now I'm a paranoid fat bitch?' I say – but I'm laughing now, because even I can see I'm getting ridiculous.

I still bow out of the meal idea even so. When I get home I tell Dad and Anna that I've eaten with Nadine. I don't hang about downstairs. I go up to my bedroom and play music and do a huge crayon drawing – a mad landscape where the sun is a giant pizza, the mountain peaks are vast cherry-tipped iced buns, the forests are fairy cakes, the rivers are bubbly strawberry milkshakes, and the grass is studded with Smarties flowers.

I go to bed early and try to sleep late because it's one way of avoiding eating times.

Anna comes into my room at ten o'clock.

'Magda's on the phone for you, Ellie.'

Oh God, what does she want at this time? I remember her big date with Mick. She probably wants to boast and give me a blow-by-blow account. I groan and get out of bed. The room suddenly spins.

'Ellie?' Anna's by my side looking worried. 'Are you all right?'

'Mmm. I just went a bit dizzy, that's all. I'm OK now.'

'You don't look OK. Are you feeling sick again?'

'A bit.'

Sick with hunger, hunger, hunger.

'Ellie . . .' Anna is staring at me, biting her lip.

'Look, I can't keep Magda waiting,' I say, pushing past her.

I don't want Anna fussing and finding out how little I've been eating. Just because she's given up on her diet it doesn't mean I've got to. And besides, Anna is skinny as anything anyway.

'Hi, Magda,' I say into the phone. 'It's a bit early, isn't it? I was trying to have a lie-in.'

'Oh. Sorry. I didn't think. I just wanted to talk to you,' says Magda. She sounds unusually subdued.

'Mags? What's up?'

'I don't want to go into details just now,' says Magda. I can hear music in the background and family noises. 'It's pandemonium here. Can I come round to your place, Ellie?'

'Yeah, OK.'

'Like . . . now?'

'Fine.'

I have a quick shower and shove on some clothes. Anna's made me tea and toast. She means to be helpful, but I'd much sooner coffee and then I can have it black and not waste calories on milk. And she's buttered my toast for me, making big yellow puddles, absolutely oozing.

'Thanks, but I seem to have gone off tea,' I say, trying to be tactful. I gnaw delicately at the crust of my toast, and then leap up thankfully when Magda rings the doorbell.

She looks awful. Her hair's brushed straight back, she's got no make-up on at all, and she's wearing an old grey fleecey thing instead of her beautiful fur coat.

'Magda? Hey, come in.' I bundle her quickly upstairs to my room so she doesn't get waylaid by Anna or Dad or Eggs. She doesn't look in the mood for socializing.

She sits on the end of my unmade bed. My Patch hot-water bottle tumbles out of my duvet. Magda sits it on her lap and strokes it absent-mindedly, as if it were a real dog. She looks like a little girl again.

'Magda?'

She starts to say something, clears her throat, tries again, fails. She shakes her head impatiently.

'What's the matter with me? I'm so desperate to tell you I get you out of bed specially – and yet now I'm here I can't get started.' She seizes Patch by the ears. 'It's Mick.'

'Yes. I sort of gathered that.'

I wait. Magda waits too. If Patch were real he'd be squealing.

'Didn't he turn up?' I prompt.

'Oh yes. Well, I watched him play his football, didn't I? Hours I stood there. It's so cold and it's so boring and I was dying for a wee but I hung on with my legs crossed and every time he came near the ball I shouted encouragement like a loony.'

'So? After?'

'He was ages getting changed, with all his mates. I just hung about. I nearly lost my temper and went home. I mean, I don't *usually* lurk outside sweaty dressing rooms for hours. And they were singing utterly infantile songs, you know the sort. But anyway, I hung on in there, and at long last out he comes, still with all the mates. And he did look pretty fabulous, in this black leather jacket, and his hair all floppy and shining because he'd just washed it. It's so unfair, how can such a creep look so drop-dead gorgeous?'

'He's a creep?'

'The lowest of the low. Because . . . well, we wandered off to the park.'

'You and Mick?'

'And all the mates. I mean, I know most of them, Jamie's OK, and I went out with Larry that time. They all seemed in a good mood, larking about, making a bit of a fuss of me, you know.'

'Well, I don't know. Not personally. But I've seen the way all the boys act when they're around you. Flies. Honeypot.'

'I certainly started to feel sticky. They had all these cans of lager – and after a while they got a bit silly. One or two of these guys started kind of mauling me about. But I thought it was all just a bit of fun. Nothing heavy. And anyway, I was sure we'd be shot of them all soon enough. I suggested to Mick that we go off for a meal. He said, "Come on, guys, Magda's hungry, let's all go to McDonald's." I didn't think this sounded very romantic and I wanted to get rid of all the mates, so I asked if we could go to a proper restaurant, just him and me. He says, "Oooh, Magda can't wait to get me on her own," in this stupid nudge-nudge wink-wink way. Larry and all the rest fall about laughing and I'm starting to get seriously pissed off by all this and so I start walking off by myself. Mick can see I'm serious and he puts his arm round me and suddenly starts to be so sweet. He apologizes and asks me where I want to go, saying we'll eat anywhere, so I suggest going to the Ruby – you know that lovely Indian restaurant with the marble elephants? I always thought it would be dead romantic to eat there on a proper date. He goes OK, for you, Magda, anything, but let's hope you're worth it . . . and I *still* didn't twig what this was all about. Oh, God.' Magda bends her head over Patch, trying not to cry.

I sit on the bed beside her and put my arm round her. I can feel her quivering.

'What *happened*, Mags?'

'I – they—'

'They didn't *rape* you?'

'No! No, I'm just making this stupid fuss over nothing. *They're* nothing. I don't know what's the matter with me. I should have just laughed in their faces. Anyway. We went to the Ruby, Mick and me. The others were still hanging around the park so I thought everything was fine. Mick was . . . he was really sweet, he said all this stuff . . . It makes me feel sick now, but I liked it at the time, I liked *him*, I thought – I thought this was really it. True Love. Oh, God. *So*, we had a couple of beers, Mick told the waiter we were eighteen, and we had a curry. Well, we shared one. It was a bit embarrassing, the waiter wasn't happy about it, but I thought maybe Mick doesn't have much cash. I started to feel mean for suggesting the Ruby. I decided I'd offer to pay myself, doing it ever so discreetly so he wouldn't be embarrassed.

'It was getting hard to think straight. I'm not really used to beer. I slipped out to the Ladies and splashed my face with cold water, and I started making all these stupid kissy-kissy faces in the mirror, thinking of Mick — and then when I came out the Ladies there he was, right in front of me, waiting for me. He kissed me and it was just amazing to start with, the way I'd imagined it would be, *better*, and he said he'd paid and said "Come on, let's get out of here," and he took me round the back to the place where people park their cars and I thought this was a bit crazy because Mick doesn't have a car and I started to tell him this but he wasn't listening, he just had hold of me practically under the arm so he could shove me along, and he got me to these trees right at the back and then — well, at first I didn't mind, he was just kissing me, I *liked* it, though I was a bit worried about my shoes because we were standing in all this leaf mould and mud, so I said couldn't we get out of the mud and he didn't understand, he took off his jacket and said I could lie on that. I said, "What do you mean, I'm not lying down," and he said, "OK, OK, standing up, fine by me," and then he pressed me back against this tree and . . . Well I just thought he was trying it on at first, and I told him to stop it, but he didn't, and his hands started going all over the place, and then he got to my jeans and I started to get mad and told him to cut it out, what sort of girl did he think I was and he said . . . he said, "Everyone knows what sort of girl you are, Magda, so stop acting hard to get, right?" and he started getting really rough then, and I got scared he really *might* rape me. I slapped his face but it just seemed to make him madder so I sort of twisted round and suddenly jammed my knee up hard and he practically fell over, grunting and groaning.'

'Good for you, Magda!'

'But then when I started running away from him and got back to the cars there were all these cheers and his mates all bobbed up and one of them said, "It's our turn now, Magda," and then Mick staggered out of the trees and he was calling me these awful names, and then they all started, and this couple came out into the car park. They'd been in the Ruby and they looked at all these boys and they looked at me, and the woman came over to me and asked me if I'd like a lift home and so I said yes. They were very nice to me, but I felt so dreadful, I knew they must be thinking I was a real little slag, just me and all those horrible drunken boys. I had my lipstick smeared all over the place and mud all up my jeans. I looked like a slag and . . . maybe I *am* a slag. That's what they kept calling me, that's what they think I am.'

'You're *not* a slag, Magda. Don't be so crazy. You're a lovely gorgeous-looking girl who went out with a total perve who got entirely the wrong idea,' I say fiercely, hugging her. 'I hope you kicked him so hard he still feels sick. How *dare* he treat you like that!'

'He said I was asking for it. He said why did I dress like a tart if I wasn't willing to act like one,' Magda sobs.

'Well, he acts like a sick creep and he talks like a sick creep and he *is* a sick creep,' I say. 'Forget him, Magda. Forget all about him.'

# Giantgirl

I go swimming on Monday morning. Zoë is there too. I hear two girls gasp as she takes off her tracksuit in the changing rooms. Zoë turns her back on them and ties her hair up in a ponytail. It hangs lankly, much thinner than it used to be.

'Zoë?' I say uncertainly. 'Zoë, you're getting *so* thin.'

'No I'm not,' she says, but she looks pleased.

'How much do you weigh?'

'I'm not sure,' says Zoë. 'Anyway I need to lose a lot more because my dad's still insisting we go away for Christmas and he'll practically *choke* me with food so I've got to be a bit on the skinny side to start with.'

'Zoë, you're not skinny, you're skeletal,' I say, but I can't persist.

Maybe she'll only think I'm jealous. Maybe I *am*.

'Is your friend Magda coming today?' Zoë asks.

'No,' I say, and my heart aches thinking about her. I forget Zoë. I forget me. I just think of Magda as I swim up and down, up and down, up and down. I can feel the adrenalin pumping in my veins. I swim faster than usual, faster than Zoë, faster than all the girls, faster than some of the boys.

There's a little crowd larking about at the shallow end. I can't see them clearly without my glasses. I'm not sure if they're any of the ones who know Mick, ones who might have been there on Saturday night.

But there's no mistaking Mick himself in the café. I go in there, hair still wet, glasses steaming up, legs bright pink from swimming, but I don't care if I look awful. I march straight up to him, sitting there with his mates. He's smirking all over his face.

'Who's this then?'

'What do you want, girlie?'

'It's Magda's mate.'

'Where's Magda then?'

'Where's Slaggie Maggie?' says Mick, and they all laugh.

My hand reaches out and I slap him really hard across the face. His head rocks in shock, his eyes popping like they're going to roll right down his cheeks.

'You shut up, you creep,' I say. 'Magda's not a slag. She's a very picky choosy girl and she'd never have a one-night stand with you or anyone else for that matter. If you dare call her names or spread rumours about her I'll tell her brothers and their mates and

119

they'll chop you stupid schoolboys into little pieces. So shut *up* about her, see?'

I storm off, the whole café staring. Some of the boys jeer, some laugh. Then they start shouting after me. They call *me* a slag. They call me Frizzy Face and Four Eyes. They call me Fat Bum. And yet I don't care. I truly don't care. I'm pleased I struck a blow for Magda. That's all that matters.

She's still very quiet and droopy at school. Nadine is also totally hang-dog because everyone naturally asks her how she got on at the *Spicy* heat and she has to say she wasn't chosen. So at lunchtime we go off by ourselves. We huddle on our favourite steps by the portakabins and we have a good long self-indulgent moan. Magda goes on about boys and what pigs they are and so why does she still fancy them? Nadine goes on about *Spicy* magazine and what a tacky tedious bore it was on Saturday so why is she still desperate to model for them? I go on about being fat and how I know it's what you are that matters, not how you look, so why am I still desperately dieting?

'But you're *not* fat, Ellie,' says Magda.

'And your diet's driving *me* bonkers the way you drool whenever I eat a bar of chocolate, so God knows what it's doing to you,' says Nadine.

'Hey! Thanks for your overwhelming sympathy and understanding,' I say. I'm sitting in the middle so I can elbow them both in the ribs. 'Look, I've been Ms Incredibly Supportive Friend to both of you. You could try being a bit sympathetic about *my* problem.'

'You haven't *got* any problems, you nutcase,' says Magda, snapping back to life.

'That's right, you're just being completely and utterly loopy,' says Nadine. 'You'll end up like Zoë if you're not careful.'

'All right, I can see Zoë's really gone a bit too far. But . . . if I could just get to be *normal* size—'

'You *are* normal! For God's sake, you keep acting like you're a freak or something, total fat-lady-in-the-circus time,' says Magda. She grabs a hank of my frizzy hair and holds it against my chin. 'You could be the Bearded Lady, easy-peasy. But fat? Forget it.'

'I *am* fat. I'm much much fatter than you two.'

'I bet we're about the same weight,' says Magda. She says how much she weighs.

It's only a few pounds less than me.

'Rubbish. You're fibbing. You can't weigh as much as that,' I say. 'Or if you really do then it's because your body's different. Heavy bones. And big muscles from all your dancing.'

'You're making me feel like a Russian shot-putter,' says Magda. 'How much do you weigh, Nadine?'

Nadine says. It's a *lot* less.

'See! Nadine's much taller too,' I say. 'I'm the squat tubby one.'

'You're the deluded nutty one,' says Magda. 'But we still love her to bits, don't we, Nadine?'

'Our old Ellie-Belly,' says Nadine, and she starts tickling my tummy.

'Don't! Get off! Stop it!' I shriek, as they both tickle me mercilessly.

121

I try to tickle them back and we roll down the steps, writhing and squealing.

Two Year Sevens scuttle past, looking as if they've stumbled on an orgy. That makes us laugh even harder. I feel so good that when Nadine produces a Twix bar I accept a bite happily. Two bites. Half the bar.

Maybe I'm going to stop dieting now. Maybe it's mad to fuss about the way I look. It's all so stupid anyway. Magda looks like a movie star and yet it just gives all those slimy sluggy schoolboys the wrong idea about her. Nadine looks like a fashion model and yet she was just one of a huge crowd of thin pretty girls on Saturday.

Maybe it's OK being me. Magda and Nadine like me. And Dan likes me too.

Dan.

What's *happened* to Dan? He sent me a funny post-card last week – but no letter. He used to write practically every day. And phone. He came down to stay one weekend. But he hasn't been back since.

I *did* tell him that he shouldn't keep bobbing up like a jack-in-the-box and we'd have to wait to see each other at Christmas. He seems to have taken me at my word.

I ask Anna when we're going to the cottage for Christmas.

'A couple of days before, I thought – just to get that awful cooking range prodded into action,' says Anna, sighing. 'Oh, God, the thought of all those lists, and all the shopping, and the packing, and the *un*packing, and then all of us shut up in that damp cottage for days—'

'I thought you *liked* going to Wales for the holidays.'

'Well. Yes. Of course I do. It's just . . . I saw Sara again today, you know, my designer friend, and *she's* spending Christmas in New York.' Anna sighs enviously. 'I mean, I wouldn't really want to swap with her, not seriously, but imagine wandering round great big luxurious shops like Bloomingdales and going up the Empire State building on Christmas Eve.'

'Imagine looking at all the Nativity paintings in the Metropolitan Museum and then going skating outdoors at the Rockefeller Centre,' I say, because I've seen them doing it in films.

We both imagine endlessly . . . and sigh.

'Tell you what,' says Anna, 'if I ever get a decent job when Eggs is a bit older – Sara says *she* can maybe fix me up with something – I'll save up and *we'll* go to New York one Christmas.'

'Dad hates flying. And Eggs would be a right pain in the shops.'

'Not them. Us. Well, we'll maybe come back for Christmas itself, I wouldn't want to be away from them then, but we could easily whizz away for a few days, just you and me.'

I feel an odd squeezing feeling inside me. I know Anna's only playing games, it's not like it'll really happen – but even so, it's weird us playing games together. We've always been on separate sides of the family. Yet now it's almost like we're best friends.

I don't mind. I *like* Anna. And yet, I think of my own mum and I feel so horribly mean to her.

'Ellie? What is it?' Anna says.

'Nothing,' I say, and I rush away quickly before I burst into tears.

I seem to be in an ultra-weepy watery mode at the moment. The last day at school is a serious strain. Oh, it's fun too, because the Sixth Form put on this special entertainment and it's seriously rude and we all fall about laughing. But when we have our last form lesson with Mrs Henderson she suddenly produces this big carrier bag and she's bought every girl in the class a little chocolate Santa. Not as big as the one Mrs Lilley offered as a prize but this is a Santa for every single girl. Sometimes the teachers give you cards but I've never had one give you presents before, especially a really strict old-fashioned teacher like Mrs Henderson.

Most of the others chomp up their chocolate straight away, a gulp of bearded head, a gollup of tummy, a crunch of boots and he's gone. I wrap mine up carefully in a hankie and put him in my schoolbag.

'For God's sake, Ellie, one little chockie isn't going to make you fat,' says Magda.

'I'm saving him for sentimental reasons, not because I'm trying to get slim.'

'Don't you overdo things, Ellie,' says Mrs Henderson, overhearing as always. 'Tuck into a few mince pies and the Christmas pud and really let rip this holiday. You can always work it off in my aerobics class in January.'

She's being so nice I almost wish I'd got *her* a present.

I *have* got a present for Mrs Lilley. Well, for little baby Lilley. I find her in the art room at lunchtime and hand it over, feeling stupidly shy as I thrust the little red crepe parcel into her hand.

'Can I peep at it now?' Mrs Lilley asks.

'OK. If you want,' I say awkwardly, wishing it was more special.

I made it in a rush in a couple of hours last night. It's a little yellow cloth teddy bear wearing a red jumper and purple trousers.

'I had buttons for his eyes at first but then I thought the baby might choke, so I sewed eyes on instead. They look a bit crossed, actually.'

'No, they don't, he just looks a bit anxious. Oh Ellie, he's *lovely*.' Mrs Lilley makes him pad about on his soft paws, acting like a little kid herself.

I'm so pleased she likes the teddy and so sad that she's going that I have to swallow hard and sniff.

'It's going to be horrible without you for Art,' I mumble.

'Ah! I think you might enjoy Art even more,' she says. 'I met your new art teacher the other day. I think you're in for a surprise.'

'Is she really nice then? Is she young? What does she look like?'

'I'm not going to say another word,' says Mrs Lilley, laughing. 'But I think your art lessons are going to be fun. You could do with a bit of fun, Ellie. You've seemed a bit down the last few weeks. There's nothing really serious troubling you, is there?'

'No. Not really. I just wish I could change myself sometimes,' I say.

'In what way?'

'Oh. You know,' I say, blushing. I wish I hadn't started this now.

I wish I could tell her how much I want to be thin. But what's the point? She'll just say something comforting about my looking fine the way I am. And I know it's stupid to be so utterly self-obsessed. I know I should start caring about heaps of other things. I *do* care about the awfulness of war and starving babies and tortured animals and destroying the countryside. It's just that if I'm totally one hundred and one percent honest I care about being fat just a weeny bit *more*.

As the teddy seems such a success I decide to revert to my old home-made habits and make everyone an appropriate soft toy for Christmas. I quite enjoy the first few days we break up from school because I go shopping for material in the market and then cut and pin and stitch for hours on end.

Eggs is a bit of a pest because he keeps wanting me to play with him, so I get him some card from a corn-flakes packet and show him how to do cross-stitch. He quite likes stabbing away at it, doing these great big wobbly crosses.

I find it helps me stop wanting to nibble all the time as you can't really eat and sew. It's annoying that it's such a sedentary occupation. I haven't been swim-ming for a bit. I'm a bit scared Mick's mates might

126

drag me right under and drown me if I dared show up. I wonder if Zoë's still going, or if she's already been hauled off for her holiday abroad? I bet she'll do aerobics up and down the aisle and refuse to eat so much as one free peanut on the plane. I don't know Zoë well enough to make her a present but if I did, her soft toy would definitely be a stick insect.

I make Magda a fluffy white cat with big blue eyes, very proud and purry looking. I tie a red satin ribbon round its neck. I make Nadine a lemur with huge black-ringed eyes, black claws and a long stripy tail.

We have a special Girls Day Out on the 22nd so we can give each other our Christmas presents. Magda and Nadine want to meet at Pizza Hut. I argue. I don't win. So I go through agonies before I order. I so badly want a pizza, a huge great deep pan four cheese pizza with garlic bread and a giant glass of Coke – and yet I add up the calories in my head and the numbers flash like pinball machines, 100, 200, 500, *1000* – and so I dither desperately.

Magda orders. Nadine orders.

'Shall I come back in a few minutes?' says the waitress, raising her eyebrows.

'No, she'll have a pizza too, with all the trimmings you've got, pineapple, pepperoni, you name it,' says Magda.

'No I won't!' I say.

'Go on, have it on me. You've got to start eating properly sometime, Ellie, it's getting to be such a *pain*.'

'You've lost heaps of weight, look,' says Nadine,

fiddling with my skirt waistband. 'Positively fading away. Have the pizza special, eh?'

'Get *off*, Nad. No. I'll have a mozzarella and tomato salad and a mineral water,' I say, although the only time I ate mozzarella cheese it was like someone had filled my mouth with soap.

I leave the cheese. I eat the tomato and the little leaves of basil and I drink my fizzy water and I'm so hungry watching Magda and Nadine I even fish out the lemon from my glass and chew up every little bit.

'Yuck, don't *do* that,' says Magda, stuffing her face with pizza.

'Honestly, Ellie, you are a prize nutter,' says Nadine, biting on a huge piece of garlic bread.

'Quit nagging me, both of you.'

'But we're *worried* about you.'

'You've got obsessed with this *stupid* diet.'

'Look, I'm fine. I'm just not very hungry, actually. Don't keep *getting* at me, both of you.'

I can't help feeling hurt. I was so supportive to Nadine. I was so supportive to Magda. Why can't they give me a bit of support for a change?

I feel so upset my tummy ties itself into a knot and I truly do lose my appetite. I put down my knife and fork and wait for Magda and Nadine to finish. They take a long time. They talk with their mouths full, their lips greasy, cheeks distorted, throats convulsing as they swallow.

'Ellie! Pack it in,' says Nadine.

'What? I'm not doing anything.'

'You're staring at me like I'm a boa constrictor and I'm eating a little bunny alive.'

'Well, come *on*. Let's do the presents.'

'When we've finished eating.'

'You have, almost.'

'Pudding!' says Magda. 'I want an ice-cream, don't you, Nadine?'

It is exquisite torture. I have always *adored* ice-cream. Maybe they're just doing this to be mean to me. The waitress brings *three* bowls of strawberry ice-cream.

'Not for me, thanks. It was only two,' I say quickly, not daring to breathe in the sweet strawberry smell.

'I signalled to her to bring three. Eat it, Ellie. Don't be such a spoilsport. You're stopping us having fun, sitting there all po-faced and plaintive,' says Magda.

'Well, if my presence bothers you that much then it's easy, I'll make myself scarce,' I say, getting up.

'Sit *down*, Ellie-phant,' says Magda.

'Don't go all snotty on us, Ellie-Belly,' says Nadine.

'No *wonder* I have a complex about my weight,' I say.

But I sit down again – and I have just one lick of the strawberry ice-cream.

It's as if a strawberry firework has exploded in my head. Another lick, another, another . . . and in less than a minute it's gone. It's so good. I can still taste it all over my tongue. But my heart is hammering. Four hundred calories? Five hundred? Plus the sauce and the whipped cream?

'Relax!' says Magda. 'Here, have your Christmas pressie. Open it now.'

She gives me this pink parcel tied with purple ribbon. It's soft and flat. I open it up – and it's a T-shirt with a picture of the famous statue Venus de Milo gorging chocolates. She's armless, so she's being fed by little fat flying cherubs. She's got a speech bubble above her head saying 'I'm the most beautiful woman in the world and I'm size sixteen – so eat up, babe!'

I laugh and give Magda a hug.

'Have mine too, Ellie,' says Nadine.

Her present is wrapped in black crepe paper tied with silver ribbon. It's very little. When I open it up I find a tiny silver elephant charm on a thin black velvet ribbon.

'It's beautiful,' I say, and I give Nadine a hug too. 'You're the two best friends in all the world. Oh, God, you've both given me such super things and I've reverted to type and done you my stupid hand-made junk again.'

'Christmas wouldn't be Christmas without Ellie's amazing hand-made junk,' says Magda. 'Come on, gimme, gimme.'

'Me too,' says Nadine.

I hand over their presents with immense trepidation but, thank goodness, they actually seem to *like* their toy animals. Magda gives her cat a big cuddle and Nadine makes her lemur climb all over the table and chairs.

Magda and Nadine swop presents too – one has an ultra posh Chanel lipstick and the other has Wolford black glossy tights – a perfect choice for each.

We all end up having a big big big hug when we say goodbye. I wish more than ever we weren't going to the boring old cottage for Christmas.

It takes for ever to load the car up the next morning. It's not just our clothes – there's all sorts of boxes and baskets full of food and drink – and *then* there's the special big box of presents. I have a little peer and prod to see what my presents might be. Looks like books, though there's a little soft parcel too, and a bigger one that rattles.

'Hey, leave that alone, Ellie!' says Dad. 'You're worse than Eggs.' He gives me a quick kiss on the cheek.

He's so happy to be off to the cottage. It's annoying but it's also kind of endearing too. He gets us singing all the crazy old Christmas songs on the journey, awful ancient things like *I Saw Mummy Kissing Santa Claus* and *Jingle Bells* and *Rudolph* and we bellow our way through all those corny Christmas hits of the Seventies and Eighties too. Eggs interrupts every five minutes to ask if we're nearly there but by the time we *are* there he's sound asleep. He doesn't even wake up when Anna lifts him out the car and staggers along the path with him to the front door.

It's raining of course, and blowing a gale too. Wonderful Welsh weather. The cottage looks exactly the same. Worse. When Dad unlocks it this damp smell oozes out as if our faces are being rubbed with an old wet flannel. Dad breathes in deeply, a great smile on his face.

'Home sweet home,' he declares, without a trace of irony.

It's not home and the smell certainly isn't sweet. Even Dad recoils from the kitchen. We forgot to throw out a bag of potatoes from last time and now they've grown so many tentacles they're like something out of *Alien*. Dad has to hold the bag of rotting spuds at arm's length as he throws it out.

Anna tries to get the stove going, hampered by Eggs, who whimpers and clings like a limpet every time she tries to put him down. We have to work hard for *hours* to restore all the ordinary necessities of life to our holiday hovel – heating, hot water, warm food and drink, aired beds – and then when we've got rid of Eggs at last and Anna and Dad and I settle down in the dreary living room with cups of stale instant coffee we find the telly's completely on the blink. There's just a roaring noise like a waterfall and a surge of little starry dots.

'Great,' I say, sighing heavily. 'And I bet there isn't a TV repair place for a hundred miles or more or if there *is* then it'll be closed for Christmas.'

'Old gloomy-guts,' says Dad, refusing to be phased. 'I'll soon fix it.'

The set remains seriously unfixed.

'Oh well, who needs boring old television any-way. We'll play games and chat and make our own amusement. We'll have a really old-fashioned family Christmas—'

'I'll look in Yellow Pages in the morning,' Anna mutters to me.

'Of course it might not be the set at all,' says Dad. 'It could be the transmitter. The line might have gone down in the heavy wind.'

'So we might be in for a total power failure,' I say. 'No telly. No heat. No light. No food.'

'Well, no food will suit you. You've hardly eaten anything for weeks,' says Dad.

He suddenly sounds serious. Anna's looking at me too. Oh, God, I can't face a Spanish Inquisition on my Eating Habits, especially not now. It's an immense relief when the phone starts ringing. I rush to answer it. It'll be Dan. I wonder when he arrived with all his family? I can't wait to catch up with all his news. It's really been ages. I wonder if his ridiculous haircut has improved any. It couldn't look *worse*.

But it isn't Dan at all. It's some sad person trying to sell double-glazing over the phone. They rabbit on before I can stop them, though it's pointless, because the cottage windows could be *triple*-glazed and it wouldn't be near lukewarm and there's no point them banging on about less noise from traffic because there's only the odd passing tractor that manages to make it halfway up this mouldy muddy mountain.

'Sorry, you're wasting your time,' I say, and I put the phone down.

'Playing hard to get with Dan?' says Dad, looking surprised. 'I thought you were getting kind of keen on him. I thought that was maybe why you'd gone into this dire droopy decline. I thought you'd chirp up as soon as he called.'

'Well, you thought wrong, didn't you,' I say. 'And as a matter of fact that *wasn't* Dan. It was someone selling double-glazing, OK? Right, as there's no telly I think I'll have an early night.'

I stomp out the room. I hear Anna groan and say, 'Why do you have to be so tactless?' and Dad moan, 'How was I to know it wasn't Dan? Why hasn't he phoned Ellie anyway?'

I don't *know* why he hasn't phoned. I thought he might try first thing Christmas Eve – but no. When Dad and Anna and Eggs are upstairs I quickly lift the receiver just to make sure the phone hasn't packed up as well as the telly. No, it's still working, and Anna does her best later on, phoning all over the place to find someone to come out and repair the television. With no luck.

'Do not despair. I'll call on Father Christmas,' says Dad, and he jumps in the car.

'*I* want to see Father Christmas, too,' Eggs clamours, but Dad makes him stay with us.

Dad is gone *ages*. Practically long enough to get to Iceland and back.

'Your dad is supposed to cook when we're at the cottage,' says Anna crossly, whipping up omelettes.

It's way past lunchtime and Eggs is driving us mad wailing that he's starving to death.

I feel I'm starving to death too. I managed to go without breakfast altogether, simply slipping my toast in my pocket when no-one was looking and then secretly chucking it in the wastebin. But Anna's omelettes are runny. If I try pocketing mine it'll seep right down my leg and into my sock. Anna makes superb omelettes – and eggs aren't *too* fattening. Though there's the milk and the butter and the cheese – and the crusty bread to go with them. Two slices.

Dad comes back at last, red in the face and ho-ho-hoing like a real Father Christmas. He's bought a brand new portable television. And four portions of fish and chips.

'But we've already eaten lunch, you silly darling,' says Anna, giving him a hug.

'I've had lunch too – a pint and a meat pie down at the pub. But it's Christmas. Let's eat two lunches,' says Dad.

Anna sees my face.

'It's all right. You don't have to, Ellie,' she says quickly.

But takeaway fish and chips have this amazingly pungent smell. My mouth waters as Dad opens up the steaming parcels. Fish and chips from the shop back in London are frequently a disappointment, limp and greasy, but the chippy down the valley is marvellous. The fish is snow-white with wonderful crispy batter and the chips are golden and salty. I try just one – and it's fatal. I end up eating my entire portion of fish and chips, and half of Eggs's too when he tires. Two and a half lunches.

As soon as I've finished I feel terrible. Utterly disgusted at my own greed and weakness. The waistband of my jeans cuts into my full-to-bursting stomach. I wish I could slice it right open so I could scrape all the food out. Well . . . I *could* get rid of it. As long as I don't hang about too long.

I can't risk the bathroom upstairs. The cottage is so small everyone's bound to hear. But there's an ancient outdoor privy we used while Dad was still organizing an indoor bathroom when we first bought the cottage. I've always been frightened of the outside toilet. There isn't a light so you have no idea if there are spiders about to scuttle all over you and you can't properly see the horrible wooden seat and its disgusting smelly hole. I've never dared sit on it properly in case any stray rats splashing around down there might suddenly want to come up for air and bite my bottom.

There's one advantage of such primitive plumbing. When I fight my way through the weeds and get in there the smell is so foul it's easy enough making myself sick. I'm heaving even before I stick a finger down my throat.

It's horrible horrible horrible while it's happening. My heart is hammering and the tears are pouring down my face. Even after it's all over I don't feel much better. I stagger weakly out into the open air and splash dubious water on my face from the old rain butt. It's not raining at the moment but the vicious wind is hopefully bringing some colour back to my cheeks.

I go indoors again, though the smell from the fish and chip papers Anna's bundling up makes me want to puke again.

'Ellie? Are you all right?'

'Mm? Yeah. Fine.'

'Where have you been?'

'I just went to use that horrid outside loo. Eggs was in the proper toilet and I was desperate,' I say. 'Has Dad got the new telly working then?'

I try to edge past her and go into the living room but Anna takes me by the arm.

'Ellie, you look awful.'

'Gee, thanks.'

'You're as white as a sheet. Have you been sick?'

'No.'

'Are you sure? You smell a bit sicky.'

'Oh, this is really Let's Flatter Ellie time. First you say I look awful and then you say I smell. Terrific.' I'm trying to joke but I feel ridiculously tearful and my mouth is starting to burble of its own accord. 'I *know* I look awful, you don't have to rub it in. I'm just a flabby fat fright, I know. No wonder Dan's gone off me, can't even be bothered to come and see me when he's just the other side of this stupid mountain, he was the one meant to be mad about me but that didn't last five minutes, did it, and now . . .'

'Now?' Anna repeats urgently.

There's a burst of cartoon music from the living room and Eggs yells triumphantly.

'Wallace and Gromit!'

'Hey, come on, you girls, come and watch the telly!'

'Come on,' I say, sniffing. 'Seeing as he's gone to such trouble to get it.'

'No. In a minute. Let's have this out now,' says Anna, hanging on to me. 'Ellie.' She takes a deep breath.

'*What?*'

'Are you going to have a baby?'

'WHAT???'

I stare at her in total astonishment.

'I've been trying to psych myself up to asking you for ages. I kept telling myself I was jumping to mad conclusions. I haven't said anything to Dad. I promise I won't breathe a word till you say it's OK. And it *is* OK. I mean, obviously it's not what anyone planned, and we'll have to consider all the options but the world isn't going to come to an end. We'll manage no matter what you decide. And it's *your* decision, Ellie, because it's *your* baby.'

'Anna. Listen. I'm not going to have a baby.'

'Well, if that's what you've decided—'

'I'm not pregnant! Anna, are you crackers or something? Baby? Me?' Then I suddenly gasp. 'Oh, God, is it because I've got so fat?'

'No! You've got *thin* over the past few weeks, but I thought that was because you were worrying – and unhappy because Dan hadn't got in touch.'

'Dan? Oh Anna, you didn't think *Dan* was the father!' The idea is so ludicrous I burst out laughing.

Anna can't help giggling too.

'Look, Dan and I haven't done anything at all. Just a few kisses, that's all. How could you think . . .?'

'I know, it did all seem so unlikely. But you must admit, you've been a bit withdrawn and moody lately, completely off your food, being sick, suddenly terrified of looking fat – and then I couldn't help noticing you haven't touched your Tampax box this month. I know you're not really regular just yet but it all started to add up. Oh Ellie, you've no idea how great it feels that I've got my sums wrong!'

She gives me a hug, but then she tenses.

'You *do* smell of sick.'

'Stop it! Don't start *again*!'

Anna holds me at arms' length and looks me straight in the eyes.

'What *is* wrong, Ellie?'

'Nothing.'

'Come on. You haven't been yourself for ages.'

'Well, good. I don't like myself. I want to be a *new* self.'

'I liked the old Ellie,' says Anna. 'You've lost some of your sparkle. You're so pale and drawn looking. I was mad to encourage you with that stupid diet. You've lost too much weight.'

'No, I haven't. I've hardly started. I'm still horribly fat, look.' I pluck at my clothes with disgust.

'*You* look,' says Anna, lifting my thick jumper.

'Get *off*, Anna,' I say, trying to pull away. 'Stop staring at me.'

'You've lost *lots* of weight. I didn't realize just how much. Oh God. Ellie, you're not anorexic, are you?'

'Of course not. Look, I eat heaps. Like two dinners today, right?'

'Yes, I suppose so. Unless . . . Ellie, you didn't deliberately make yourself sick, did you?'

My heart is thumping but I manage to meet her eyes.

'Honestly, Anna, give it a rest. First I'm pregnant, then I'm anorexic, then bulimic!'

'Sorry, sorry. I'm making a complete mess of all this. Look, the Dan situation. You say you're not friends any more?'

'I don't know. I don't know what the situation *is* because I haven't seen Dan for ages.'

'Are you two women going to stay gassing in this kitchen all day long?' says Dad, putting his head round the door. 'Come and watch the new telly now I've got it.'

'OK, OK, we're coming.'

'And you'll be seeing Dan soon enough,' says Dad. 'I bumped into his dad in the pub. I invited the whole family over for a Christmas drink this evening!'

# Chapter Eight

## Familygirl

# Familygirl

'You've done *what*?' I say to Dad.

'I thought you'd be pleased,' says Dad, bewildered. 'You've been dying to see young Dan, haven't you?'

'No! Well . . . the point is, I wanted *him* to get in touch with *me*. Now he'll think this is all my idea. Oh Dad, how could you?'

'Yes, how *could* you?' says Anna. 'You idiot! Christmas drinks? What drinks? We've only got wine for the meal tomorrow and a few cans of beer. And then there's all their kids. How many are there, five, six? And what about *food*? We'll have to give them snacks of some sort. I've got one jumbo bag of crisps and one tin of peanuts. They'll wolf them down in one gulp.'

'Is Dan coming, Dad? I like Dan. He plays good games and makes me laugh,' says Eggs.

'Yes, pal. Dan is coming. I'm glad *someone's* pleased.' He hoists Eggs onto his shoulder and they go back to the television.

'I'm not going to be here when they come,' I insist. 'I'll go out.'

'Don't be daft, Ellie. Where can you go? You can't tramp up and down the mountain in the dark.'

'But it'll look so gross. Oh God, if I stay *I'll* look gross. I haven't brought any of my decent clothes with me.'

'Neither have I. Still, Dan's family aren't exactly stylish dressers.'

We both have a catty giggle. They are dedicated anorak wearers.

'So what *are* we going to give them to eat?' Anna says, looking through the cardboard boxes in the kitchen. 'I'll have to drive down to the village and raid the Spar shelves. Honestly. As if I haven't got enough to do. I was going to get all the veg prepared and stuff the turkey ready for tomorrow.'

'I'll get started on all that,' I say.

I scrub potatoes and peel sprouts and stuff turkey until my hands are sore. Then I dab at my face in the freezing bathroom and try to pull my hair into place. I pull on my black jeans and my black and silver shirt. My stomach still seems bloated and I'm scared they won't fit – but I can button the jeans easily and the shirt doesn't pull across my chest the way it used to. So I must have lost weight. Quite a lot . . .

Anna is really grateful when she gets back from her trip to Spar, and even more so when I grill little sausages and fill vol-au-vent cases and wrap brown bread around tinned asparagus spears. I arrange them ultra-decoratively, making little faces with wedges of cheese and pineapple and olives on crackers for the children. I don't have as much as one nibble although I'm feeling a bit faint – but I get a weird little thrill out of this. I'm in control now. I'm getting thinner. I'M GETTING THINNER!

But I feel fatter-fatter-fatter when I hear the car draw up outside the cottage and the slam of doors and lots of voices.

Anna, Dad and Eggs go to the front door. I hang back, trying to look cool.

Dan's brothers and sisters pour in, wearing hand-knitted old jumpers and baggy dungarees. There are far more than I remembered – some have got friends with them. It's a good job Anna did her Spar trek. Then Dan's mum and dad come in and they're wearing matching sheep sweaters and jeans that go in and out in all the wrong places. They've got friends too – a man with yet another jolly jumper (manic woolly frogs) and smelly old cords, and a droopy woman in a patchwork waistcoat and an Indian skirt with an uneven hem.

Then another stranger comes in. A girl about my age. Another refugee from the Style Police. She's wearing a man's rugby shirt and saggy tracksuit bottoms. There's a lot of bottom in the bottoms. She's not exactly fat – just big all over, and brawny with it. There are serious muscles under those stripes. She's got long hair that looks even frizzier than mine but it's scraped back in a schoolgirly plait so tight it's making her forehead pulse. She smiles.

'Hi there, folks.'

Oh, God. She's even heartier than I thought. Who is she?

'I'm Gail,' she says, waggling her fat fingers. 'I'm Dan's friend.'

I stare at her. The whole room goes suddenly quiet. Waiting. Dan himself makes his entrance. He trips over the doormat, staggers dramatically, and is about to go headlong but Gail catches his arm and yanks him upright.

'Whoops!' she says.

'Whoops indeed,' Dad mutters, suddenly by my side. 'Hey Ellie, what are you drinking, sweetheart? Coke? Orange juice? Tiny drop of wine?'

He is being sweetly supportive, even offering me a chance to drown my sorrows.

'Ellie, can you pass round some of the plates? Ellie did all the food. Hasn't she done it artistically?' says Anna, forcing everyone in the room to nod admiringly.

Dan is standing still, red in the face, but his eyes are gleaming behind his steamed-up glasses. His severe crewcut has grown into a strange scrubbing brush that defies gravity. Gail grins and ruffles his bristles affectionately.

'Honestly, Danny, you are a fool.'

Dan certainly looks a fool. He's wearing a man's rugby shirt too. The shoulders droop at his elbows, the hem flaps round his knees. It is sadly obvious that this is a virgin rugby shirt that has never seen action on a muddy field. Perhaps Gail has another kind of action in mind. She can hardly keep her hands off him.

Eggs does his best to elbow her out of the way.

'Hi, Dan, hi! It's me! Eggs!'

'Hi, Eggs,' Dan says, and he picks him up and turns him upside down and tickles him.

Eggs squeals and wriggles and kicks. One of his feet catches Gail right in the stomach. Anyone else would double up, but she seems to be made of india rubber.

'Hey, little sprog! Watch those Kickers!' she says, and she takes him from Dan and shakes him.

It's good-humoured and if it was Dan Eggs would adore it — but he stiffens instead.

'Stop it! Put me down! You'll make me sick!' he screams.

Gail puts him back on his feet, her eyebrows raised.

'Hey, calm down! You're fine,' she says.

Eggs ignores her. He looks straight at Dan.

'Who *is* that girl?'

'That's Gail. She's my friend,' says Dan.

'Do you mean your *girlfriend*?'

'Hey, hey, Eggs, that's enough,' says Anna. 'Come over here.' She can't remove him physically because she's balancing three platefuls of food and her hands are working overtime as it is.

Dan shuffles in his plimsolls. Gail is nowhere near as reticent.

'Sure, I'm Dan's girlfriend,' she announces.

'No you're not,' Eggs says, outraged. '*Ellie's* Dan's girlfriend, not you.'

'Shut *up*, Eggs,' I say, backing against the wall.

Eggs won't shut up.

'Why can't Ellie still be your girlfriend? She's much nicer,' Eggs insists.

'Button it, Eggs,' says Dad, and he whisks him up and takes him upstairs.

Eggs remains unbuttoned, shrieking as he goes. There's a terrible silence downstairs.

Oh God. Everyone's trying very hard indeed to pretend I'm not here.

'Who'd like a vol-au-vent?' Anna says desperately.

'I'll fetch some more,' I gabble and rush out to the kitchen.

I lean against the sink and pour myself a glass of water. I gulp it, trying to calm down.

'Ellie?'

I splutter. Dan has followed me into the kitchen.

'Are you OK?'

I've got water dribbling out of my nose and he asks me if I'm OK! Dan thumps me hard on the back.

'Hey! Don't!'

'Sorry, sorry, I just thought you might be choking.'

'Well I'm not. And it should be me thumping you, not the other way round.'

'Oh I'm sorry, Ellie. I didn't know what to *do*. I thought I'd just sort of fade out of the picture. It would be easier for everyone, right? I thought you'd maybe sussed things out already, and anyway, it was always me crazy about you, not the other way round.

147

I thought we'd maybe not even meet up – but then your dad invited us all, and *my* dad said it would look ever so rude if Gail and I didn't come too. I felt awful. I mean, it wasn't like I was trying to flaunt Gail in front of you. Even though I'm so crackers about her now you're still my *first* girlfriend and – and – and I know I should have told you about her but I kept putting it off and—'

'Dan. Stop burbling. It's not like we were ever a real *item*. It's no big deal. Honestly.'

Am I just saying this or do I really mean it? Dan is a good mate but I was mad to think I could ever nurse a grand passion for him. Or a weeny passion. Or any passion at all.

If Gail was a slender stylish sort of girl then I'd feel horrible. But she's like a cartoon version of me – only even fatter. Built like a tank, in fact. With the same knack of squashing people flat. She comes bounding into the kitchen even though it's obvious Dan and I need five minutes together to sort things out in private.

'No hard feelings, eh, Ellie?' she says, clapping me on the shoulder.

I'll have a large bruise there tomorrow.

She insists on telling me this long and totally dreary tale of how they met. She was part of a girls' rugby team playing a match at Dan's school and he provided the oranges at half time. Oh please, is this *romance*? Then they saw each other on a bus and Dan was just bowled over. Apparently. Anyway, what do I care?

I really *don't* care. And yet . . . even though Dan is

such a totally sad case it feels a bit weird not to have anyone at all now. I originally invented a relationship between us just to kid on to Magda and Nadine that I had a proper boyfriend at long last. After they found out I went through a stage of thinking maybe Dan could still be a boyfriend. He looks a complete idiot and acts like it too but he *can* be bright and funny and inventive. Occasionally. And he always had this one redeeming feature. He treated me like I was Juliet and he was Romeo.

Only now it turns out I was just his Rosaline. *Gail* is Juliet. They're acting out their major love scene right in front of my eyes. They're hardly Leonardo di Caprio and Claire Danes, granted. But when they look into each other's eyes and laugh it's as if they're in a little world of their own. And everyone crammed into our mouldy cottage belongs to someone else and I suddenly feel so lonely, because I'm on my own and I haven't got anyone – not even Dan.

There's one good thing. I feel so out of it that I don't even feel hungry. I pass plates of food round and round the room and I hand out glass after glass of drinks but the only thing I have all evening is water from the tap. No calories at all.

Anna dodges out to the kitchen and comes up to me.

'I think you're being marvellous, Ellie.'

'It's just as well you don't still think I'm pregnant,' I say. 'Oh Anna, imagine Dan being a dad. He'd wrap a nappy round its head and tie a bib on its bottom.'

Anna and I laugh, all girls together. Half an hour

later I see Dad hold up this corny bunch of mistletoe and they kiss like love's young dream. I feel so lonely again. So totally out of it that the social smile stiffens on my face and tears prick my eyes.

I know what I want to do. I want to phone my girlfriends. But the phone is in the living room and all these people are milling about talking and kids are dashing around all over the place and it's simply not possible.

'Ellie?' Dad leaves Anna and comes over to me. 'Ellie, are you all right?'

'No. I'm all wrong.'

Dad drops the mistletoe onto the carpet.

'I'm sorry. This is all my fault. I'm an idiot. What can I do to make it up to you?'

'Make them all vanish so I can phone Nadine and Magda.'

'Mmm. I'll try,' he says. He wiggles his nose, shuts his eyes, and mumbles, 'Hocus pocus, Gobblede-gook, Please disappear when I next have a look.'

'Er . . . it hasn't worked, Dad.'

'True. Do you really badly want to phone Magda and Nadine?'

'Yes. But I can't. Not in front of everyone.'

'Well, I'm Father Christmas, right? So shove a coat on and come and have a ride on my sleigh.'

Dad takes my hand and we slip out of the house. He drives me down to the village, parks outside the public phone box, and presents me with his own phone card.

'Oh, Dad! Hey, you're *my* Father Christmas.

150

Thanks ever so,' I say, giving him a hug.

I phone Nadine first.

'Oh Ellie, I'm going completely off my head,' Nadine whispers. 'My aunty and uncle and my gran are all here and the curly-haired lisping infant is showing off till it makes me sick and everyone keeps nagging me to cheer up because it's Christmas. It's the total pits.'

I soothe in sisterly fashion, and reassure her that I'm actually having a *worse* time, with my ex-boyfriend parading his new girlfriend at my party.

Then I phone Magda and she's got a party going on at her house too.

'But I just can't get into the party mood somehow,' Magda says. 'There's several really tasty-looking boys, my brothers' mates, and normally I'd be bouncing about in my element but since that awful night with Mick I'm kind of scared. I don't want anyone else to get the wrong impression, so I've just been really quiet and hardly talking to them and my entire family keep telling me to cheer up because it's Christmas and I'm, like, *so*?'

'I've just phoned Nadine and she feels exactly the same way.'

'Well, at least you're OK, Ellie. You've got Dan and *he's* hardly likely to leap on top of you and then spread filthy stories about you. He's a total sweetie even if he's a bit of a berk. Oh sorry, I didn't mean that the way it sounds.'

'Feel free to insult him all you like, Magda,' I say, and I tell her about Dan and his new love.

We end up having a really good laugh about it until Dad's phone card runs out.

'That was a *great* Christmas present,' I say.

I get some great real presents the next day too – a book on Frida Kahlo, *The Bell Jar* by Sylvia Plath, *The Color Purple* by Alice Walker, a stylish black designer swimming costume and a big box of very expensive artists' chalks – all from Dad and Anna. Eggs gives me a new sketch book. I spend most of Christmas morning doing a portrait of each of them.

We're playing Happy Families.

But then it all goes wrong.

We sit down to Christmas dinner around two o'clock. I've told Anna I want a really small portion but all the plates are piled high. She sees me looking anxious.

'Just leave what you don't want, Ellie,' she says, trying to keep the peace.

It's not that easy. Once my teeth get started they won't stop. It's truly delicious: large glistening golden turkey with chestnut stuffing and cranberry sauce, little chipolatas and bacon rolls, roast potatoes, sprouts, parsnips, beans. I eat and eat and eat, and it tastes so good I can't put my knife and fork down, I cut and spear and munch until every morsel is gone. I even wipe my finger round my plate to savour up the last smear of gravy.

'Ellie! You'll be licking your plate next,' says Dad, but he's smiling. 'It's great to see you've got your appetite back.'

I don't stop there. The mince pies were all eaten at

the party last night but there's still Christmas pudding with brandy butter, and then I have a tangerine, and then three chocolates with my coffee.

'Glug glug,' says Eggs, downing a cherry brandy liqueur chocolate.

'Oh God!' says Anna. 'Spit it out at once, Eggs!'

Eggs swallows, his eyes sparkling.

'Am I drunk now? Ooh, goodee! Am I going to sing silly stuff like Dan's dad did last night?'

'You sing silly stuff without being drunk,' says Anna. 'Don't you dare touch any more of those liqueur chocolates.'

'That's not fair. You let Ellie.'

'Well, Ellie's nearly grown up.'

I'm not so sure. I don't know whether it's the half glass of champagne at the start of the meal or the three chocs at the end, but I'm starting to feel seriously woozy. My stomach hurts I've stretched it so much. I put my hands on it gingerly. It's huge, like I'm suddenly six months pregnant.

I suddenly panic. What am I *playing* at, stuffing myself with all this food? I must have put on pounds and pounds. I've messed up all the past weeks of careful dieting.

I've got to do something about it. Quick.

'I feel like a bit of fresh air,' I say, getting up from the table.

'Hang on. We'll just tackle the dishes and then we'll all go for a walk,' says Dad.

'No, I feel all funny. I'm just going outside for a bit. Leave the dishes. I'll help with them later,' I say.

153

I rush out without even stopping to grab a coat.

'Ellie?' says Dad.

'She's drunk!' Eggs declares. 'Um! Ellie's drunk.'

I do feel drunk as the icy air hits me. The mountain moves, the woods waver, the little brick privy fades in and out of vision. I feel sick. Thank God, it's going to be easy.

I breathe in deeply inside the loo. I retch at the smell. I get ready, tuck my hair back behind my ears, shove two fingers down my throat.

It all happens in a rush and a roar. My eyes are tightly shut, tears seeping down my cheeks. Then I hear someone gasp. I open my eyes and see Anna peering round the door at me.

'Anna! Leave . . . me . . . alone!' I gasp.

She's waiting outside when I stagger out.

'What the hell are you doing to yourself, Ellie?'

My heart pounds. I hold my neck. My throat's so sore now. I'm trembling.

'I was being sick, that's all. Don't look at me like that. I couldn't help it. It's because I ate so much. The chocolates must have been the last straw.'

'Don't lie, Ellie. I followed you. I saw what you were doing.'

'You followed me into the lavatory? What sort of weird snoopy act is that?'

'I care about you, Ellie. I've let you pull the wool over my eyes these past weeks but now we've got to sort this out. We're going to talk it over with your father.'

'Now? For God's sake, Anna, it's Christmas Day.'

'Yes, and it was the Christmas dinner I spent all morning cooking on that awful stove, and it all turned out OK in the end, and I was so thrilled when you ate it all up so appreciatively, and we were having such a lovely time and then, *then* you go and spoil everything.'

'I was sick. That's not my fault.'

'You liar! I saw you put your fingers down your throat.'

'OK, OK, I felt sick and I just needed to help myself—'

'You're bulimic, Ellie. You did it yesterday too. I knew you had, but you kept lying to me. *Why* are you doing this? It's so mad. I can't understand how anyone could want to make themselves sick.'

'I don't enjoy it! It's awful. But what else can I do when I'm so weak-willed and eat myself silly. I've *got* to get rid of all that extra food before it makes me even fatter.'

'But you're *not* fat.'

'I *am*. Horribly fat.'

'You're not, you're not!'

'What on earth are you two doing out there?' Dad calls from the open kitchen door. 'Why are you shouting at each other? Come indoors, you're both shivering. What is it? What's happened?'

We go in. Anna starts. I tell her to leave it for another time. Dad tries to lighten things up, but Anna insists he listen to her. She says all this stupid stuff about me, exaggerating heaps. I'm *not* bulimic. I've made myself sick three times, that's all. No big deal.

And I'm not anorexic either, though Anna insists I'm that too.

'Ellie can't have that slimming disease thingy,' says Eggs. 'She isn't thin, she's fat.'

'See!' I say, and I burst into tears.

Anna says Eggs doesn't really mean fat. Eggs says he does. Anna tells Eggs to be quiet. Eggs says it's not fair. *He* bursts into tears. Dad says this is ridiculous, it's Christmas, and he's bought this brand new television and now nobody's watching it and why did Anna have to start this stupid row. Anna says she's desperately concerned about me and Dad ought to be a better father and she's sick to death of worrying about me and *she* bursts into tears. Dad says we're all getting upset about nothing and of course Ellie isn't really anorexic or bulimic and neither is she fat and there's nothing to worry about and let's stop all this nonsense and make the most of Christmas.

So we try.

Thank God for the television. There's a good film on and after a few snuffles and sighs and wounded glances we all get absorbed. We're almost playing Happy Families again – but then it's teatime.

I daren't risk starting eating again in case I can't stop. So I just sit there quietly, sipping a cup of Earl Grey tea with lemon, doing nobody any harm.

'Ellie! You're not eating,' says Anna.

'I still feel a bit sick.'

'Don't start now.'

'I *do*.'

'Have some of this yummy Christmas cake. Look,

156

this bit's got extra icing,' Dad says heartily, as if I'm Eggs's age.

'I don't want any cake, thank you,' I say, though the rich moist fruity smell is making my mouth water. I especially like the icing, that lovely crisp bite in and then the sweetness spreading over the tongue blended with the odd almondy tang of marzipan.

'How about just a tiny slice if you've really not got any appetite?' says Dad.

I could eat a huge slice. Two. I could eat the entire cake in one go, for goodness' sake.

'I'm really not hungry.'

Anna sighs. 'OK. No cake. But your stomach is completely empty now. You must eat something. A slice of bread and butter – and some fresh fruit – and a slither of cheese.'

She cleverly arranges a dainty slice of bread on a plate and puts a Cox's apple and a few green grapes and a slice of brie beside it.

'Hardly any calories, and it's all good wholesome nourishing food,' she says.

It's so tempting – but my total splurge at lunchtime has scared me. Once I start I won't stop. It'll be another slice of bread and then another, more fruit, all the brie, then I'll get started on the stilton . . .

'No thank you,' I say primly, pushing the plate away.

'Oh for God's sake, Ellie,' says Dad. 'Eat the damn food.'

'No.'

'Look, you're acting so childishly. Just eat it.'

'I don't want to.'

'Then get down from the table and stop spoiling Christmas tea for everybody else,' says Dad.

'Certainly,' I say, and I march out of the room.

Anna is crying again. I feel guilty. She was trying to be kind. But I can't help it. I'm not being difficult on purpose. I've been a positive saint this Christmas helping with all the cooking and not throwing a tantrum when Dan paraded his girlfriend before me. I'm not demanding special treatment or my own diet. I tried to be as discreet as possible when I was sick. It's not my fault Anna came snooping after me. Why can't they all just leave me alone?

Dad comes to talk to me.

'Leave me alone.'

Anna comes to talk to me.

'Leave me alone.'

So I am left alone for the entire evening. I can hear them downstairs laughing at something on the television. I take my new chalks and my new sketch book and draw a table groaning with Christmas fare. But it's all been spoilt – there's furry mould growing on the sandwiches, the fruit is rotting in the bowl, little mice are nibbling the cheese, and flies crawl all over the white icing on the cake.

# Chapter Nine

# Problemgirl

A pattern sets in. I don't eat. Anna cries. Dad shouts. I go to my room and draw. I don't eat. Anna cries. Dad shouts.

I go to my room and draw . . .

Eggs stays on the sidelines.

'You're mad, Ellie,' he says, slurping chocolate in front of me.

'She's driving us all mad,' says Dad. 'For God's sake, Ellie, how can you be so selfish and self-obsessed? You're just playing for attention.'

'I don't want attention. I want to be left alone.'

'It's all my fault,' says Anna.

'What?'

'I was the one who suggested a diet in the first place. It was crazy of me. And then it's been hard for Ellie, losing her mother and having to get used to a stepmother. I think it's partly symbolic. Ellie and I have got closer recently and this is worrying for her. She must feel she's being disloyal to her mother's memory. So she rejects my food. It's a way of rejecting all my nurturing and care.'

'I've never heard such silly rubbish,' says Dad. 'I can't stomach that psychological claptrap. Don't you start blaming yourself, Anna! You've been great with Ellie. Look, she's just gone on a diet and got obsessed with it, that's all. She's got nothing else to think about while she's here. And she's probably brooding about the Dan situation – which I didn't help, I know.'

They're both so *wrong*. It's certainly nothing to do with Dan. We saw them when we were out for a very wet walk. Dan and Gail were wearing matching orange cagoules, hoods pulled low over the forehead. They were clasping woolly gloves and striding out in step, left, right, left, right. They might have been made for each other. I must have been mad ever to think Dan might have been made for *me*.

It's not anything to do with Anna either, although that gets to me more. I feel guilty about Anna. I don't want to make her so worried about me. I didn't realize I could bother her so much. And fancy her saying that about my real mum! I never talk about Mum to anyone. Dad thinks I've forgotten all about her.

I'll never forget. I still talk to her sometimes in my head. I've got her photo on my bedside table at home but I didn't bring it to the cottage. I suddenly long to see it. I try drawing Mum from memory but it doesn't work out too well. The line falters as I try to sketch her chest, her waist, her hips. I've always thought my mum looked beautiful – long dark properly curly hair, not frizzy like mine. Big dark eyes, heart-shaped face, soft cheeks, soft white arms, soft cushiony breasts – I can still just about remember the way she used to cuddle me when she put me to bed. But now I think of her soft curvy body and I wonder. Was my mum a little bit fat? Not as fat as me, of course, but still pretty chubby.

I try to remember what she looked like without any clothes. I must have seen her in her bath, or pottering around the bedroom in her bra and knickers? I feel bad, as if I'm snooping through a keyhole at her. What does it matter if she was fat or thin? This is my dead mother, for heaven's sake.

I don't believe in heaven but I draw a child's version of it, all snowy clouds and golden gateways and I seat my mum on a special starry throne, decked out in a spangly robe and designer wings in sunset shades. Just for a moment her sweet chalk face softens in a smile and she says 'What does it matter if *you're* fat or thin, Ellie?'

I know she's right and I try to hang on to this. Maybe if she and I were by ourselves in the cottage we'd have a meal together and we'd laugh and talk and eat, no trouble at all. But when Dad insists I come down for dinner he's all bossy and blustering.

'Now stop this silly nonsense right now, Ellie. You're going to clear your plate, do you hear me?'

Anna is all tense and tearful.

'I've fixed you a special salad, Ellie, and there's cottage cheese, no calories at all. You can just have a tangerine for pudding – just so long as you eat *something.*'

Eggs is ultra-irritating.

'I'm eating all my turkey pie and all my mashed potatoes and all my sweetcorn and *then* I'm eating all my ice-cream because it's yummy and I want it in my tummy. I'm good, aren't I, not like silly smelly Ellie belly who's still f-a-t even if she *is* on this stupid diet.'

How can I relax and say, 'OK, folks, drama over, I'll eat normally now?'

So I don't eat (apart from a few mouthfuls that I chew for ages and sometimes manage to spit into my paper hankie) and Anna cries and Dad shouts and I go to my room and draw.

'Thank you for spoiling Christmas for everyone, Ellie,' says Dad as we drive home. He's gripping the steering wheel so fiercely he'll rip it right out of the dashboard in a minute.

'I didn't do anything. I don't know why you're being so horrible to me.'

'Now listen to me, young lady. I'm making a doctor's appointment for you the minute we get home, do you hear me?'

'You're shouting so hard the whole *motorway* can hear you.'

'I've just about had *enough* of you and your wise-crack answers and your pained face and pursed lips at the dinner table and your sheer bloody obstinacy. You've not eaten properly for days. *Weeks.* You're making yourself ill. It's dangerous to lose so much weight so quickly. You look a complete wreck, all gaunt and pale and ghostly, like some poor soul with a terminal illness.'

Do I *really* look gaunt? I try to see myself in Dad's driving mirror. I suck in my cheeks hopefully but it's useless, I look as round and roly-poly as always, baby cheeks and chubby chin.

'I suppose you think you look soulful and interesting,' says Dad, catching my eye in the mirror. 'Well, you don't, you look dreadful. And you're so undernourished you're coming out in spots.'

'Thanks a bunch, Dad,' I say, feeling a hundred suppurating boils erupt all over my face.

I *had* been feeling a bit mean because I know how much Christmas at the cottage means to Dad, and he'd tried to be really sweet, buying the little telly and taking me down to the phone box so I could chat to Nadine and Magda but now he's being so horrid I don't care at all if he feels I mucked up his Christmas. *Good.* I can't stick him. He can't force me to go to the doctor. It's *my* body and I can do what I want with it.

I can't be bothered unpacking and doing any of the boring stuff when we get home. Why should I help Dad and Anna when they just nag at me all the time? I rush to the bathroom, take off my shoes and my jeans and my heavy bangle and weigh myself. Wow. I really have lost weight. Of course I'm still *fat*. I stare at myself sideways on in the bathroom mirror, hiking up my shirt to get a proper peek at my tum and bum and OK, I'm maybe a *weeny* bit smaller but I'm still huge. But not *quite* as huge as I was. Still a lot fatter than Magda, and totally gross compared with Nadine. But improving. I wonder if Nadine and Magda will notice?

I phone them. Magda first.

'Let's meet up, right? *Not* my place, it's all doom and gloom with my family,' I hiss. 'What about the Soda Fountain?' I could just have a fizzy mineral water, no problem.

'No, not the Soda Fountain,' Magda says quickly. 'Let's go somewhere . . . quiet. How about upstairs in John Wiltshire's?'

'What?' John Wiltshire's is this dreary old department store where all these grannies meet for a cup of tea. 'Are you kidding, Mags?'

'No. They have luscious cakes. Or are you still dieting?'

'Well. Sort of,' I say casually. 'OK, John Wiltshire's will be fine with me if that's what you want. Four o'clock? I'll phone Nadine, right?'

Nadine sounds a bit odd too. Very subdued.

'Are you OK, Nad?'

'No,' says Nadine.

I can hear Natasha in the background, squealing and giggling, and Nadine's mother clapping and clucking at her.

'Family life getting you down?'

'Understatement of the century,' says Nadine. 'Oh Ellie, wait till you hear. I can't bear it!'

'*What?*'

'No. I can't tell you properly now, not with you-know-who around. I'll tell you when we meet up, right? Only don't say I told you so, *please.*'

'Promise. Four o'clock, John Wiltshire's. I can't wait!'

But when we meet up we're both so distracted by Magda we forget Nadine's revelations. My weight loss goes unremarked. We are just utterly *jawpunched* by Magda's appearance.

I don't even *recognize* her at first. I spot Nadine hunched at one of the twee pink-clothed tables with some mousey short-haired girl in a grey jacket. Then this same girl smiles wanly at me. I do a triple take.

'Magda! What have you *done*?'

Nadine signals to me frantically with her eyebrows.

'You look so different, but – but it looks . . . great,' I lie desperately.

'It looks totally crappy and so do I,' says Magda, and she bursts into tears.

'Oh Mags, don't,' I say, putting my arms round her.

I stare down at her poor shorn head. It isn't just the new brutal haircut. It's the colour. Magda's been a bright bottle-blonde right from our first day in Year Seven when she was eleven years old. I've never been able to picture her any other way. But now she's had it dyed back to what is presumably her natural pale brown. Only it doesn't look natural on Magda. She looks like she's taken off her own jaunty flowery sunhat and borrowed an old lady's 'Rainmate' by mistake.

Nadine orders us all pots of Earl Grey and toasted

teacakes. I am so distracted by Magda I munch teacake absent-mindedly. It's only when I'm licking the butter from my lips that I realize I've chomped my way through hundreds of unnecessary calories. Oh, God. I wonder about a quick dash to the Ladies but the cubicles will be in full earshot of everyone, and I don't want to miss out on anything when Magda and Nadine spill the beans.

'Sorry about the snivelling,' says Magda, wiping her eyes. She's not wearing any make-up either, so she looks oddly unfinished, as if someone has already wiped half her face away.

'Your hair really looks quite . . . cute when you get used to it,' I try again.

'That sort of gamine look is actually very hip now,' says Nadine.

'You liars,' says Magda. 'It looks awful. And the colour is the end too. Not even mouse, more like moulting hamster with terminal disease. I'm going to get it dyed again before school but how the hell can I grow it again in a week?' She tugs at the limp little locks in despair.

'So – *why*, Magda?' says Nadine. 'Did the dye go wrong so you had to cut it all off or what?'

'Or what indeed,' said Magda. 'No, it was just . . . Oh, it's so stupid. I thought I was over that night with Mick, you know, but I went into town last Saturday – remember I phoned you and asked you to come, Nadine, but you said you were busy?'

'Don't!' says Nadine. 'Oh, God, I wish I *had* come with you. Anyway. Go on.'

167

'And you were still stuck in Wales, Ellie,but I thought never mind, I'll go round the sales anyway, as I had lots of lovely Christmas lolly to spend. I went with my brother Steve because his girlfriend Lisa works at the Virgin record store so she's tied up on Saturdays and so Steve and I had a good look round the Flowerfields Shopping Centre and I got some new shoes and he did too and we went into *La Senza*, you know, that nice nightie place, and I bought this cute little nightshirt with teddies on and Steve bought this cream lacey negligee for Lisa because she'd said she liked it ages ago and now it was down to half price. Anyway, we were a bit tired by this time and I was wearing my new shoes and they were making my feet ache a bit so Steve suggested we go and have a milkshake in the Soda Fountain and . . .'

'Were Mick and his mates there?'

'Not Mick himself, but some of those guys he hangs out with, Larry and Jamie and several others. I sat right the other side with Steve and we were just clowning around. You know what fun our Steve can be. He took Lisa's negligee out of the carrier and held it up against himself, and I was laughing away at him when I suddenly looked up and all these boys were staring at me and then they all started mouthing *Slag* at me and I just about died.'

'Oh Magda, you mustn't take any notice of them. They're just pathetic scum,' I say fiercely.

'But I just couldn't stand the way they were looking at Steve and me. They'd obviously got completely the wrong end of the stick.'

'You should have told your Steve.'

'Yes, and he'd be banged up for grievous bodily harm right this minute. Anyway, I tried to work out *why* all these boys have got the wrong idea about me.'

'It's simple, you nutcase. You look a million dollars!'

Used to look a million dollars. Now it's down to thousands. Hundreds. Several dollars.

Magda reads my expression. 'Exactly. It was my blond hair and the make-up and the showy clothes. So I thought, right, I'll stop being blond, so I went to this hairdresser with the rest of my Christmas dosh and said I wanted it all cut off and dyed back to its original colour. They didn't think it a very good idea, but I insisted. Oh, God, why am I such a fool? Look at it!' She runs her hands through her hair.

'It'll grow,' says Nadine. 'Give it another month or so and it'll look great, you'll see. And maybe you can go back to being blonde again. I can't quite get used to you as a brunette, Magda.'

'And what's with this old grey jacket? You've got a red fur coat to die for,' I say. 'Honestly, Magda, I think you've had half your brain cut off as well as all your hair. How can you possibly let a sad little bunch of schoolboy prats affect the way you look?'

'Hello?' says Nadine. 'Do you hear what you're saying, Ellie? Just one kid calls you fat at that *Spicy* mag do and you go totally anorexic overnight.'

'That's nonsense,' I say, blushing hotly. I didn't realize Nadine actually *heard*. 'And I'm not anorexic. Look, I've just eaten a huge great buttery teacake. I bet that's 400 calories gone for a burton already.'

'You're *proving* my case,' says Nadine. 'And look at yourself, Ellie. You really are getting much thinner.' She flattens my sweater against my stomach. 'Look Mags. The incredible shrinking girl.'

'Oh, Ellie. *You're* mad too. It doesn't suit you going all skinny,' says Magda.

Skinny! Ow wow. SKINNY! I'm not, of course. I've still got a long long long way to go before I could possibly be called skinny. But still . . .

'You've no idea how scary this is,' says Nadine. 'It's like my two best friends have been taken over by aliens. *The X-Files* have got nothing on this.'

'*You* looked different the day you went to the *Spicy* girl heat.'

'Don't remind me,' says Nadine, and she flicks her last piece of teacake in my face.

'So anyway, what's with you, Nad? What was this seriously awful thing that happened to you?'

'Oh God,' said Nadine. 'Do I have to?'

'Yes!'

'Well, it's just . . . last Saturday, when I couldn't see you, Magda, it was because I went up to town to this place.'

'What place?'

'A studio.'

'Oh no! A photographer's studio? You went to see that creepy guy who gave you his card, didn't you? Oh Nadine, you nutcase. What did he try to do? Did he want to take sleazy glamour shots?'

'No, he didn't, Ms Clever Dick. He took entirely

respectable totally fully-clothed photos,' says Nadine. 'I've got a proper portfolio. And he did only charge me half price. Though I hadn't realized quite how much it would be. It used up all my Christmas present money.'

'So what's the big deal?' says Magda. 'That's good, isn't it?'

'That's the good part. The bad part – the truly infuriating awful part – was that my mum and my horrible little showy-offy sister came with me. Mum caught me sneaking off on Saturday morning, see, and wanted to know where I was going and asked why did I deliberately make myself look a sight wearing all the black and the goth make-up and stuff, I looked a total laughing stock. She was being really irritating, totally getting at me and trying to put me down, so I found myself telling her I'd been invited to this special fashion photo session. It was just to shut her up, which was crazy because as soon as I'd got her convinced she started insisting she had to come too. She jumped to just the same sort of conclusions as you two. She said she had to be like a chaperone and said I couldn't go at all if I didn't let her come along too. So I had to give in – but *that* meant Natasha tagging along as well because my dad had this boring old golf match—'

'So did Natasha show off and start her Shirley Temple stuff and embarrass you at the studio?'

'Worse. Far worse,' says Nadine. 'She was feeling sick from the bus journey when we first got there so she just lolled against Mum and said nothing at all, like she was all sweet and shy. She kept staring at me with her beady little eyes. I felt so weird standing there under all the hot lights. And all my make-up started running too. I'd really gone a bit mad with it, you should have seen the eye make-up but that was a big mistake too. He said I'd maybe overdone the goth look.'

'But he *told* you to stick to your own style.'

'Yes, but he said I'd taken him a bit too literally and that anyway, fashions were changing. The little junkie weirdo look *had* been big in magazines but now the buzz word is wholesome. So, you can imagine how I felt, and, of course, I couldn't whip all the make up and clothes off and start all over again. He said it didn't matter, I still looked ever so striking, and he started taking my photo but it didn't really work. "Give me some oomph, babe," he kept saying.'

'What a berk.'

'No, I knew what he meant, that sort of special sparkly look like a light bulb has suddenly been switched on inside your head but mine seemed to have gone 'phut'. I mean, how can you slink about and smile sexily in front of your mother and your kid sister? You just feel stupid. Especially as I looked all wrong. I think these photos are going to be a total disaster.'

'Then that's his fault,' I insist.

'No. Wait. At the end, when he could see we really weren't getting anywhere, he said we might as well call it a day, and he said he had a few photos left at the end of the reel. He asked my mum if she'd like several family shots thrown in as a little extra or maybe a couple of the little girl, seeing as she'd been so good.'

'Oh-oh,' I said. 'I can guess what's coming next.'

'That's it. You've got it. Natasha stood up in front of the camera and it wasn't just a light bulb switching on. She blazed like a beacon with fireworks fizzing out of her ears. She smiled and she pouted and she wiggled and she giggled and the photographer suddenly went crazy. He forgot all about me. He started an entire new reel of film and he took *endless* photos of Natasha and burbled away at her and didn't once have to tell her to give him some oomph. She had so much of it she blasted me right out of the studio.'

'Oh Nad. I'm sure your photos will be just as good. Better.'

'Rubbish, Ellie. Of course Mum was over the moon at all this and happily forked out for Natasha's portfolio even though she isn't paying a penny of mine, which seems horribly mean to me. The photographer guy says he knows this woman who runs a kids' modelling agency and he's going to drop off some contact prints to her and he's pretty sure she'll be very interested in Natasha.'

'Oh *yuck*.'

'Double triple quadruple yuck,' says Nadine.

'Hey, don't be so mean to poor little Natasha, you guys,' says Magda.

We both elbow her indignantly. Magda has always had this annoying blind spot where Natasha and Eggs are concerned. She can't seem to see how irritating it is to have little pests for kid sisters and brothers. She thinks they're *cute*.

'You know what else he said? He said it was not only great to discover such a natural little beauty as Natasha – *natural*, Mum puts her hair up into little kinks each night just so she can flounce those awful ringlet curls around during the day – but he also said she was so unspoilt and ultra-well-behaved that he thought any modelling agency would welcome her on to their books.'

'And he didn't say anything about getting you into any agency, Nad?'

'Did he hell. So, my career seems to have fizzled out before I've even got started.'

'We haven't had a fun time this Christmas, any of us,' I say. 'Magda's had too much attention from boys and so now she's trying to look like one—'

'That's not true!' says Magda. 'Anyway, Ellie, you maybe haven't had *enough* attention so you're starving yourself to death to get everyone to take notice of you.'

'Oh, don't you start on the psychological tack. Anna's been bad enough coming up with all these weird and wonderful reasons why she thinks I'm doing it. She can't seem to understand that I just want to lose a bit of weight. That's all. Why does it have to be such a big deal?'

To my horror *Dad* suddenly goes all psychological on me too. He buys this paperback about teenage eating disorders and he sits with his nose buried in it, getting gloomier and gloomier as he turns the pages. Every now and then he gives a little groan.

I do my best to ignore him but he comes over to me, looking anguished.

'Ellie, can we have a little chat?'

'Oh, Dad, don't start again, please! Look, I ate a huge tea, a vast plate of scrambled eggs on toast, so quit nagging me.'

'You ate about three forkfuls. And you left both slices of toast on your plate.'

'Well, they went soggy and you know I can't stand soggy toast.'

'You've always got an answer for everything, haven't you? That's exactly what this book says.'

'Oh, *Dad*. Why do you have to take any notice of that stupid old book?'

'It's worrying me, Ellie. You really do have all the classic signs of an anorexic personality. You're clever, you're a perfectionist, you're very determined, you can lie like crazy, you've had a traumatic childhood . . . you know, losing your mother so young.' Dad's voice has gone wobbly. He'll never talk about my mum, even now.

There's something else bothering him too.

'Ellie, would you say we get on OK, you and me?' he asks gruffly.

'No! We're always arguing,' I say.

His face crumples. I suddenly feel awful.

'Oh, Dad. Don't look like that. I didn't really mean it. Look, *all* teenage girls argue with their dads. But we get on fine most of the time, I suppose.'

'Would you say I was very authoritarian? You couldn't possibly, could you? I mean, I'm usually quite a hip sort of Dad, right? I don't boss you around that much, do I? Ellie? Oh for goodness' sake, put those chalks down and look at me! I'm *not* authoritarian, am I?'

'Listen to yourself, Dad!'

'Oh, come on, give me a break,' says Dad. He's still not finished. He clears his throat. 'Ellie . . .'

'Mm?'

'Ellie . . . it says in this book that anorexia can also be a response to abuse.'

'What?'

'Some poor girls have horrible abusing fathers.'

'Oh *Dad*. *You're* not a horrible abusing father! Don't be so daft!'

'Remember that time when Eggs was just starting to toddle and I saw you push him over so that he bumped his head? I smacked your bottom then. You howled and howled, remember, and I felt terrible because I'd never laid a finger on you before.'

'Dad, that was years and years ago! Look, just because I'm on a diet it's got nothing at all to do with you – or anyone else for that matter.'

'But this isn't just a simple diet, Ellie. How much weight have you lost since you started to get obsessed?'

'I'm *not* obsessed. And anyway, it's only a few pounds.'

'I had a word with Dr Wentworth—'

'*Dad!* I *told* you, I'm not going to see her. There's nothing wrong with me.'

'She asked if you'd lost ten per cent of your body weight – and *I* don't know.'

'Well I do,' I say firmly. 'I haven't lost that much weight, Dad, honestly.'

I'm being anything but honest. I really seem to have got the knack of dieting now. I'm still starving hungry all the time and my tummy aches badly and I keep having to pee a lot and whenever I get up quickly or rush round I feel faint and most of the time I've got a headache and I feel a bit sick and I've got a filthy taste in my mouth and my hair's gone all floppy and I've got spots all over my face and on my back too – but it's worth it to lose weight. Isn't it? I'm not anorexic. Not like Zoë.

I wonder how she's getting on? I bet her dad's nagging her too!

I can't wait to see Zoë on the first day back at school. Will she have put on any weight or will she be even thinner?

Lots of the girls in my class notice that *I've* lost weight.

'Wow, Ellie! You're looking so different!'

'Look at the waistband of your skirt. It's hanging off you!'

'Have you been ill or something, Ellie?'

'What's the *matter* with you, Ellie?'

'*Nothing's* the matter. I've just been on this diet, that's all.'

'A *diet*? Over Christmas? You must be mad.'

'Catch me going on a diet! We went to my nan's and she does all this home baking. Oh, her Christmas cake! And her mince pies – I ate *five* in one day.'

They burble on about food and I find it so irritating I open up my desk and start rearranging all my school books, trying to ignore them.

There's a sudden shriek – a scream – an entire operatic *chorus*.

'Magda!'

'Look at *Magda*.'

'Magda, your *hair*!'

Oh, God, poor Magda. No wonder they're all going berserk. Maybe the newly shorn mousey Magda won't be able to shut them up. I bob up from my desk, ready to spring to Magda's defence.

I spot Magda.

*I* squeal.

She's not the old bouncy blonde. She's not the new subdued mouse. She's an utterly new sizzling scarlet Magda!

Her hair's a wonderful vibrant electric bright red, the exact shade of her beautiful fur jacket. It's been cut even shorter, but in brilliant elfin-punk layers like flaming feathers.

Magda looks totally *incredible*. And she knows it. She grins at me.

'I hated my new look so I decided to go for an even newer one,' she says. 'You were so right, Ellie. Why should I scuttle round like a colourless creep just because of those sad bastards. I want to be *me* again.'

'Well, well, Magda!' says Mrs Henderson, bustling

into the classroom. 'I think I'm going to need sunglasses to look at your new hairdo. That is *not* an appropriate colour for school. If I were in a bad mood I'd make you cover it up with a headscarf but mercifully for you I'm feeling *mellow*.' She smiles benignly. 'Did you have a good Christmas, girls?' She catches sight of me. 'Oh dear, Ellie. You did *not* have a good Christmas. You've obviously been starving yourself, you silly girl.'

'I'm just getting fit, Mrs Henderson. I thought you'd approve,' I say, secretly thrilled.

Mrs Henderson is frowning at me. 'You and I had better have a private chinwag later, Ellie.'

Then Nadine comes into the classroom – and Mrs Henderson is diverted. Her mouth actually drops open. The entire class stares, jaws gaping.

Nadine hasn't changed her hairstyle.

She hasn't changed her weight.

She's changed her *face*.

She stands nonchalantly in the doorway, the wintery sunlight full on her face. She has a tattoo! A long black snake starts at her temple and writhes right across her forehead and down one cheek, the tip of its tail ending in a wiggle at her chin.

'Dear goodness, girl, what have you *done* to yourself?' Mrs Henderson gasps.

'Nadine! That is so—'

'Amazing!'

'Gross!'

'Disgusting!'

'Incredible!'

179

'Super-cool!'

Nadine, the amazing gross disgusting incredible super-cool snake woman, grins at us all and then puts her hand to her forehead. She pulls – and the snake wriggles right off her face and hangs limply from her fingers.

'Father Christmas put a joke tattoo in my stocking,' she says, while we all scream at her.

'You bad bad girl,' says Mrs Henderson. 'My mellow mood is rapidly disappearing. I feel as if I need another holiday already!'

She's a good sport all the same but I'm going to do my best to keep out of her way the next few days. I don't like the sound of this private chinwag.

We have a morning assembly as it's the first day of term. I crane my neck looking for Zoë but I can't see her anywhere. Maybe she's still abroad with her family?

Magda gives me a nudge.

'Hey, who's the dishy dreamboat on the stage?' she whispers.

'He can't be a teacher!' says Nadine.

We have three male teachers already. Mr Prescott takes us for History. He looks as if he's stepped straight out of the Victorian age, and acts it too. He's stern, stiff, uptight and *ancient*. Mr Daleford is the IT teacher, with all the warmth and charisma of his own beloved computers. He even talks like a Dalek. And Mr Pargiter teaches French. He's quite sweet but very balding, very tubby and very middle-aged so he's not exactly dreamboat category.

The man on the stage is youngish, definitely still in his twenties. He's got tousled dark-blond hair which looks wonderful with his black clothes – black button-down shirt, thin black tie, black jeans, black boots.

'This is Mr Windsor, girls – our new Art teacher,' says the head.

Mr Windsor shyly nods his blond head. Every girl in the hall stares transfixed. *Wow!*

# Chapter Ten

# Portraitgirl

We can't wait for our first Art lesson.

Mr Windsor talks for ages about Art, his eyes shining (dark brown, a beautiful contrast to his blond hair). He shows us these reproductions of his favourite paintings, whizzing through the centuries so he can tell us about the different techniques and styles. He also throws in a lot of interesting stuff about the painters themselves and their lifestyles.

'Yeah, it was fine for *them*, all these painter *guys*,' says Magda. 'But what about women artists? They didn't get a look-in, did they? I mean, you call all this lot Old Masters, don't you, so where are the Old Mistresses?'

'Ah! You're obviously a fierce feminist and you've got a jolly good point too,' he says, smiling at the newly-gorgeous scarlet Magda.

She's not a feminist at all. I don't think she cares tuppence about Art either. She just wants Mr Windsor to take notice of her, and it's certainly worked.

So then he goes on about the secondary role of women artists through the ages, starting off with nuns in convents poring over illuminated manuscripts. Then he tells us about a female artist called Artemisia Gentileschi who was raped and he shows us this amazing painting she did of Judith cutting off this guy's head, with blood spurting everywhere. Lots of the girls shudder and go 'yuck' but Nadine cranes forward to take a closer look as she's into anything seriously gory. She's applied her joke snake tattoo to her arm now, so that the forked-tongue snake's head wiggles out of her school blouse and down across her hand.

Mr Windsor spots this and admires it. He flicks through a big book on sixties pop art and holds up this picture of an astonishing model called Snake Woman. She's got snakes coiling round her head like living scarves, and her body is all over scales.

'And it's by a woman too,' he says, grinning at Magda.

I'm getting to feel horribly left out and let down. I'm the one who's mad keen on Art and yet I can't think of a single thing to say. He holds up a picture of Frida Kahlo and it's the very one I've got pinned up in my bedroom at home. I can't really put up my hand and announce this – I'll sound so wet. So I listen while he talks about Frida and her savage

South American art. I nod passionately at everything he says. Eventually he sees this and looks at me expectantly.

'Do you like Frida Kahlo's work?'

Here's my chance. I swallow, ready to say something, *anything* – and in the sudden silence my tummy suddenly rumbles. Everyone hears. All the girls around me snigger. My face flushes the colour of Magda's hair.

'It sounds as if you're ready for your lunch,' says Mr Windsor.

He waits for me to comment. I can't. So he starts talking about another artist called Paula Rego. I just about die. My stupid stomach goes *on* rumbling. There's nothing I can do about it. Why can't it shut up? He'll think I'm just this awful greedy girl who wants to stuff her face every five minutes. It's not fair. I've been so careful recently, totally in control. I've only eaten a few mouthfuls at every meal. I didn't even have breakfast this morning, *or* any supper last night.

Which is why my stomach is rumbling.

Why I feel so sick.

Why I feel so tired I can't think of a thing to say.

Why I keep missing out on what Mr Windsor is saying. It's really interesting too. I hadn't even heard of Paula Rego before. She's done all these extraordinary pictures in chalk. I can tell by the colours in his big book of reproductions that they're just like my new Christmas present pastels. She does pictures of women unlike anything I've ever seen before.

They are big women, ugly women, in odd contorted positions.

'Why does she paint women like that? They look awful,' says Magda.

'I don't think they look awful. I think they're incredible,' says Mr Windsor. 'Maybe they look awful to you because we've all become so conditioned to think women should only look a certain way. Think of all the well-known portraits of women. The women are all prettified in passive poses, the body extended so that all the bulges are smoothed out. The face is frequently a blank mask, no lines, no tension, no character at all. These are lively expressive real women, standing awkwardly, stretching, dancing, doing all sorts of things.'

'But they're *fat*,' I whisper.

Mr Windsor reads my lips.

'You girls! You're all brain-washed. They're big women, they're strong, they've got sturdy thighs, real muscles in their arms and legs. But they're soft too, they're vulnerable, they're valiant. They're not beautiful women. So what? Beauty is just fashion. Male artists have used beautiful women throughout the centuries but their sizes and proportions keep changing. If you were Giovanni Annolfini in the Middle Ages then your ideal pin-up girl had a high forehead and a tiny bosom and a great big tummy. A century later Titian liked large firm women with big bottoms. Rubens liked his women large too, but wobbly. Goya's women were white and slender, then Renoir liked them very big and salmon pink.'

'And Picasso liked his ladies with eyes in the side of their heads!' says Magda, and we all laugh, Mr Windsor too.

Why can't it be *me* making him laugh? I rack my brains for something to say . . . but I'm running out of time. The bell goes before I can come up with anything.

Mr Windsor sets us all Art homework.

'I want you all to do a self portrait. You can use any medium you like. Don't forget to bring it with you next time, right? When do we meet up for Art again?'

Next Friday. I can't wait. We spend the next lesson whispering about the wondrous Mr Windsor.

'Isn't he fantastic?' says Magda.

'He's got such a lovely sense of humour too,' says Nadine.

'It's OK for you two. You both made a big impression on him. I just made a right idiot of myself,' I wail.

'You should have spoken up for yourself,' says Magda.

'You should have told him that you and Zoë did all the mural. That would have impressed him,' says Nadine.

'I couldn't just announce the fact. It would look like I was showing off,' I say.

I wonder if Mr Windsor might like Zoë and me to do some special artwork like Mrs Lilley used to? I still haven't see Zoë. At lunchtime I go to Mrs Henderson's aerobics class to catch Zoë there.

Lots of girls in lycra shorts are bobbing up and

down but Zoë isn't one of them. I join in anyway though I find it horribly hard going. I have to stop several times to lean against the wall and gasp for breath. I don't seem to be getting any fitter. Is it because I'm still far too fat? Or is it because I've tried to get thin too quickly? My head spins. I can't think straight any more.

'Are you all right, Ellie?' Mrs Henderson asks at the end of the class.

'I'm . . . fine,' I gasp.

'Are you kidding yourself? Because you're certainly not kidding me,' says Mrs Henderson. 'Ellie, how am I going to make you see sense? I'm so worried about you. I think I'm going to get in touch with your parents.'

'No, don't, please! There's nothing wrong with me, Mrs Henderson, honestly.'

'You're obviously starving yourself.'

'No, I'm not. I eat heaps, honestly I do.'

'Oh, Ellie. This is a nightmare. It's the Zoë situation all over again. She wouldn't listen to reason either and now she's in hospital.'

'Why? What's the matter with her?'

'You know perfectly well she's anorexic.'

'But it's not an illness!'

'Of course it is. And now Zoë has made herself so dangerously ill she's had to be hospitalized. She collapsed over Christmas. She very nearly died of heart failure.'

It's so scary I can hardly take it in. I ask Mrs Henderson which hospital Zoë's in, and after school

I phone Anna and tell her I've got to go and visit a sick friend so I won't be home till late.

I hate the hospital. My heart starts pounding as soon as I get off the bus and see the big red building with its tower and chimney and endless odd extensions, like a perverted version of a fairy castle. People always go on about hospital smells but it's hospital *colour* that I can't stand. There are hideous orange plastic chairs in the waiting areas. I remember sitting hunched up on one for hours, sucking my way through an entire packet of fruit gums, whining for my mother. Who was somewhere I wasn't allowed to go. Dying.

Orange is supposed to be a cheerful colour but it always makes me want to cry. I feel tearful now, which is silly, because my mother died years and years ago. And Zoë isn't going to die – is she? I don't even know her that well, it's not like she's my best friend like Nadine and Magda. I suppose she's the girl I identify with most. So maybe I'm scared *I'm* going to die. Which is completely mad. I'm not too thin, I'm still really grossly fat.

It takes me ages to track Zoë down. I'm told she's in Skylark ward but when I get there and tiptoe past all these pale patients lying listlessly on their pillows I can't find her anywhere. There's one empty bed and I start to panic, thinking she really has died but when I eventually find a nurse she says that now Zoë's heart condition is stabilized she's been transferred to Nightingale ward in the annexe across the road.

I've heard of Nightingale. It's the psychiatric unit.

If one of the girls is acting extra loopy at school then people say she'll end up in Nightingale. The local nuthouse. Once we were in the car near the hospital and I saw a large wild-eyed woman running down the road in her nylon nightie and fur-trimmed slippers and Dad said she was obviously legging it out of Nightingale.

I remember her red sweaty face and the spittle drooling down her chin. What are they doing, shutting Zoë up with a lot of mad people? She's not *mad*.

I'm scared of going into the Nightingale building. I'm not even sure they'll let me in. Maybe they don't allow visitors.

But I force myself to go and see. There are people wandering round the grounds. No-one's wearing nightclothes. No-one looks particularly mad or distressed. Maybe they're not patients, maybe they're visitors or staff? Or maybe Nightingale isn't a psychiatric ward any more? There aren't any locked gates at the entrance to the ward. I can go right in.

An old man is leaning against the wall. He's saying something but when I look at him he hides his face, still mumbling into his fingers. A woman bustles past, walking too fast, biting the back of her hand agitatedly. Oh, God. It's the psychiatric ward all right.

I peer round, expecting mad-eyed maniacs to come hopping down the corridor in straitjackets but the people here seem sad rather than mad and they're not really frightening. I proceed up the corridor nervously until I get to the nursing station.

'Can I help?' says a woman in a T-shirt and jeans.

191

I can't work out if she's another patient or a nurse out of uniform. I mumble Zoë's name.

'Ah yes. She's upstairs, in the room at the end. I'm not sure how she feels about visitors at the moment. I think it might be family only.'

'That's OK, I'm her sister,' I lie smoothly, surprising myself.

'Oh. Well, I suppose that's all right,' she says doubtfully. 'You are over fourteen, aren't you?'

'Oh yes,' I say, and I make for the stairs before she can stop me.

I understand why Zoë's upstairs when I get to this new ward. It's as if it's a planet peopled by a strange new sisterhood. Painfully thin girls are sitting watching television, dancing jerkily to pop music, exercising in baggy tracksuits, flicking through magazines, huddling in high-necked sweaters, crying in corners. It's not just their skeletal state that makes them look alike. They've all got withdrawn absorbed expressions on their faces as if they're watching television screens inside their own heads. Even when they talk to each other they have a zombie look. It's like they're all under the same enchanted spell.

For one moment it works on me too. I look enviously at their high cheekbones and fragile wrists and colt-like knees, feeling grotesquely fat and lumbering in their ethereal presence. But then a nurse walks past carrying a tray – a lively looking young woman with shiny bobbed hair and a curvy waist and a spring to her step. She's not thin, she's not fat, she's just a normally nourished healthy person. I look at her and then I look at all the anorexic patients.

I see them clearly. I see their thin lank hair, their pale spotty skin, their sunken cheeks, their sad stick limbs, the skeletal inward curve of their hips, the ugly spikiness of their elbows, their hunched posture. I see the full haunted horror of their illness.

'Who are you looking for?' says the nurse.

'Zoë. Er – I'm her sister.'

'Pull the other one,' says the nurse, but she smiles. 'She's not feeling very co-operative so she's not supposed to have visitors at the moment but maybe you'll do her good. She's in the cubicle at the end.'

I approach the drawn curtains apprehensively. You can't knock on a curtain. I clear my throat instead, and then call out.

'Zoë?'

There's no answer.

'Zoë?' I say a little louder.

I peep round the curtain. Zoë is lying on her bed, curled up like a baby, her head tucked down on her chest. The bones at the top of her spine jut out alarmingly. She is even thinner, so small and sad and sick that I'm not shy any more.

'Hi, Zoë,' I say, and I sit on her bed.

She looks round, startled. She frowns when she sees it's me.

'What are you doing here?' she says fiercely.

'I – I just came to see how you are,' I say, taken aback by her aggression.

'How did you know they'd shoved me in here?'

'Mrs Henderson told me.'

'That nosy old busybody. So I suppose she's been telling everyone that I'm in the nuthouse.'

'No! Just me. Because – because we're friends.'

'No, we're not. Not really. Look, I don't want to see anyone, not like this. I look so awful. They're practically force-feeding me. I know I've put on pounds and pounds since I've been here. I'm getting so *fat*.' She clenches her fist and punches her own poor concave stomach.

'Zoë! Don't be crazy. You're thin – terribly thin.'

'But not as thin as I was.'

'Thinner. Much thinner. That's why you're here. Zoë, you nearly *died*. You had a heart attack or something.'

'It was just because I took too many laxatives, that's all. I'm fine now. Well, I would be if they'd only let me *out*. They've given me this absolutely ridiculous target weight. They want to blow me right up into an elephant.'

'They just want you to get better.'

'It's all right for you to talk. You're looking really thin yourself, Ellie. You're OK. You're not forced to eat huge mounds of mashed potato and drink great mugs of milk.'

'Come off it. I'm still huge compared to you. So's everyone. Zoë, you're not seeing things straight. *Look* at yourself.' I pick up her stick arm, terrified my fingers might poke right through her papery skin. 'You're literally skin and bone. You're starving yourself to *death*.'

'Good. I don't want to live. There's absolutely no

point, not like this, when everyone's against me and my parents keep yelling at me or they cry and they just won't understand, and all the nurses spy on me in case I can hide some of the food and they even ration my *water* now, just because I drink a lot before I get weighed. What sort of a life is it when I can't even go to the toilet without a nurse hanging round outside, listening?'

'So why can't you eat a bit? Then you can come out of hospital and get back to school. Zoë, listen, there's this fabulous new Art master, Mr Windsor, he's really young and good-looking, and he's great at telling you all sorts of things about Art. I made a bit of a fool of myself in our first Art lesson actually, it was dead embarrassing—'

But Zoë isn't listening. She's not interested in a new teacher, or Art, or me. She's not able to think of anything else in the whole world but starving herself.

She curls up in her ball again, her eyes shut.

'Do you want me to go, Zoë?'

She nods.

I reach out and touch the awful unpadded jut of her hip. She jumps at my touch.

'Goodbye Zoë. I'll come back again soon, if you don't mind,' I say, patting her gently.

A tear dribbles from under her closed eyelids.

I'm in tears myself as I walk down the ward. The nurse looks at me sympathetically.

'Did she give you a hard time? You mustn't take it personally. Poor Zoë thinks we're all conspiring against her at the moment.'

'Will she get better?'

The nurse sighs. 'I hope so. I don't know. We try to get the girls to a healthier weight and they have group therapy and individual counselling but so much depends on the girls themselves. Some of them get completely better. Some recover for a while but then go spiralling downwards. And others—'

'Do they . . . die?'

'It's inevitable after a certain stage. The body burns up all its fat and then starts on the muscle. The girls know what they're doing but they can't stop it.'

I can stop it. I can't stop Zoë. But I can stop myself getting to be like her.

I still feel fat, even though I've lost weight. I'd still like to be really thin. But I don't want to be sick. I don't want to starve.

I go home. Anna is full of questions but she can see I can't really bear to talk about it. She's prepared a salad for tea.

'Oh boring. I want chips,' says Eggs.

'You can have crisps with your salad,' says Anna.

She doesn't say so, but this is a carefully chosen special meal for me: fromage frais, strawberries, avocado, rocket and raddiccio. Anna is darting little apprehensive looks at me. I nibble my lip. My head is automatically calculating calories, panicking at the avocado. I put my hand up to my forehead to try to stop it. I look at the plate of lovingly prepared nourishing food, so carefully arranged in rings of red and green around the snowy fromage frais.

'This looks lovely, Anna,' I say. 'Thank you very much.'

I start to eat it. I bite. I chew. I swallow. Eggs is chattering but Anna and Dad are silent. Watching. Practically holding their breath.

'It's OK,' I say. 'I'm not going to hide bits in my lap. I'm not going to spit it into my hankie. I'm not going to make myself sick.'

'Thank God!' says Dad. 'Oh Ellie. I can't believe it. You're actually eating!'

'I'm eating too!' says Eggs. 'I *always* eat and yet no-one makes a fuss of me. We don't have to have special salads for Ellie every day, do we?'

'Of course we do,' I say, but I wink at Anna to show I'm joking.

Dad gets all fussed and suspicious when I make for the stairs straight after tea.

'Where are you off to, then?'

'I'm going to do my *homework*, Dad. Honestly.'

I'm telling the truth. Well, I'm not that fussed about my French homework. And I'm going to have to bribe Magda to do my Maths for me tomorrow morning. But I spend all evening on my Art homework, attempting a self portrait.

I don't just do one, I do half a dozen and they're all hopeless. I peer into the mirror and I still see this fat frizzy-haired girl staring back at me. When I draw her she gets even fatter and she's frowning, looking like she's about to burst into tears.

There's a knock on the door. Anna.

'OK, Ellie? I've just put Eggs to bed. Your dad

and I are having a coffee. Want one?'

'Yes, please.'

She comes in the room when she hears me sigh.

'What's up? Oh, Ellie, these are so *good*!'

'No, they're not. I look hideous.'

'You've made yourself look much fatter than you are – and you don't look very *happy*.'

'No wonder. I can't draw for toffee,' I say, and I crumple them all up.

'Oh don't! They were so good. Show your dad.'

'No. I'll have another go tomorrow.' I rub my eyes. 'I'm tired.'

'Me too.'

'Anna – thanks for being so nice.'

It's a silly inadequate little word. Our English teacher always has a fit if I put it in an essay. But Anna smiles as if I've declared an entire poem of praise.

She *is* nice. I'll never love her the way I love my own mother. But if I can't have my mum maybe Anna's the next best thing.

I go downstairs for my coffee. I have one of Anna's home-made cookies too, savouring every mouthful. I'm scared I'll want another and another, eating until I've emptied the tin.

No. I don't have to binge. I don't have to starve. I don't want to end up one of those sad sick girls in Zoë's ward. I'm going to eat what I want, when I want. I can do it. I *can*.

I sleep soundly for the first time in ages and wake up early, feeling full of energy. I feel like a swim but I can't, because of Mick and all his horrible friends.

I *can*. I'm not going to let those idiots stop me doing what I want.

I put my swimming costume on under my school uniform and grab a towel. Anna is in the kitchen buttering rolls.

'I don't want breakfast, Anna.'

'What?' She looks stricken.

'Only because I'm going swimming. I'll take a roll with me and eat if after, OK?'

'OK,' says Anna.

I don't know if she totally trusts me. I'm not even sure I trust myself. I stride out towards the swimming pool but as I get nearer I start to feel sick. There's every chance Mick and his mates will be there. I don't know what they're going to say to me, do to me. I slapped his face hard last time. There'll be a lifeguard on duty so they can't really drag me into the pool and drown me but they can still say stuff.

If they called Magda a slag they'll think up something far worse for me. I'm shivering now. I must be mad. I *can't* go swimming.

I can, I can, I can.

I pay, I go in the changing room, I take off my clothes. I fiddle desperately with my new swimming costume, pulling it down over my bottom, then haul it up to cover more of my chest, tugging it this way and that. I still feel so fat, even though I'm thinner than I've ever been before. I feel my figure in the dark of the changing cubicle. I think of poor Zoë and her desperate delusion that *she's* fat, even though she's a five-stone skeleton.

'I'm not fat,' I whisper. 'I think I am, but I'm not, and even if I *am*, it doesn't matter, it's not worth dying for. Now, I'm going to get out there in the pool. Who cares if anyone sneers at me in my swimming costume? Mick's mates can call me the fattest stupidest slag in the world and I shall take no notice whatsoever.'

I walk out determinedly, taking purposeful strides, my head held high. The effect is ruined when I trip over someone's flip-flop sandals and nearly fall flat on my face. I jump in the pool and start swimming so no-one gets a chance to stare at me. I can't see properly without my glasses. I have no idea whether Mick's mates are here or not. I gradually get into the rhythm of my swim and stop worrying so much. It feels so good to stretch and kick and glide.

There's a cluster of boys braying with laughter at the other end of the pool. I'm not sure whether it's *them* or not – or if *I'm* the butt of their joke. But I swim up to the end and back and no-one grabs me, ducks me, tears at my costume. They don't even come near me. It can't be the same boys. Thank goodness.

I don't want to try my luck too far. I get out the pool sharpish and go and shower, tingling all over, feeling so good. I whistle as I towel myself dry and pull my clothes over my damp skin. I feel Anna's roll in a bag in the pocket of my blazer. I take it out and munch it gratefully while I'm drying my hair.

I could do with a drink too. I've got money on me. I could go and have a quick hot chocolate in the café.

Those boys are still larking around in the pool. They won't be out for ages yet.

Oh God, hot chocolate! My mouth's watering.

I make for the café and order myself a hot chocolate with cream. The smell of it makes me feel weak. I spoon a little of the frothy cream into my mouth and savour the sweetness. Then I take a long swallow of the warm smooth chocolate. It is *so* good, the most beautiful drink in the world. I drain the last delicious drop and get up to go. I get to the door of the café – and collide with Mick.

Oh help! I'd better get away quick. I dart forward and he ducks.

Hey! He thinks I'm going to give him another slapping!

'You watch it,' he says gruffly, keeping well out of my reach.

'*You* watch it!' I say.

He glances round to see if any of his mates are about. No. It's just the two of us. And he's acting like he's really scared of me!

I grin triumphantly and march outside. I feel like singing and dancing and punching the air. I got the better of *him* all right. I didn't let him push me around. *I* did the pushing.

I feel so p–o–w–e–r–f–u–l.

That's the look I want for my self portrait. I use dark pastels and big bold strokes for this seventh attempt. I make my hair frizz with life, I stick my chest right out, I stand with my fists clenched and my legs spread out. I work and work at it, adding highlights here, smudging and softening there. My eyes are aching and my hand has got cramp by the time I'm satisfied.

It's the best thing I've ever done.

I hope Mr Windsor likes it. Well, *I* like it, even if he doesn't. That's what really matters. That's what I tell myself anyway. But I feel stupidly anxious when it's Mr Windsor's Art lesson.

He draws his own self portrait to start things off, taking a black felt tip and squiggling it all over the page in a matter of seconds. We all laugh when we see the way he's done it. He's drawn a big cardboard cut-out super-cool man in black – but it's being held up like a shield in front of a nervous looking boy-man with a twitchy face and knocking knees.

Then he asks to see our portraits. Magda's first, waving her picture right in his face. She's copied a curvy black and white Betty Boop cartoon, adding her own face crowned with her new startling crop.

'I like it, Magda, especially the head,' he says. 'But you above all need the full technicolour treatment. Paints!'

He gets a pot of scarlet poster paint and dips in his brush.

'Do you mind, Magda?' he asks.

'Be my guest!'

He does several deft flicks with the tip of his brush so that the paper Magda sprouts fantastic flaming-red hair.

'Wow! How about nails and lipstick to match?' says Magda.

Mr Windsor colours her to perfection. He even does little scarlet hearts all over her dress. Then he dilutes the red to the palest pink and shows us how to get a good natural skin tone.

'Though someone's just complimented Magda on her hair so she's blushing a little,' he says, putting more colour in her cheeks.

Magda's own cheeks are pink with pleasure when he gives her back her portrait.

'Who's going next?' asks Mr Windsor.

There's a general clamour. Portraits flap in the air like flags. Mr Windsor picks at random.

Not me.

Not me.

Not me.

Nadine. Her turn. She's drawn herself very long, very lean, very Gothic Queen.

'Yes, Nadine, you've got a very elegant line – practically Aubrey Beardsley,' he says. 'I don't think we should colour you in. You're very much a black and white girl. Ah! You were the girl wearing the joke tattoo. Shall we indulge in a little skin art?'

'Yes, please!'

Mr Windsor takes his black felt tip and does the most wonderful swirly intricate tattoos up and down Nadine's drawing's arms and then he takes a special silvery pen and gives her a sparkly nose stud and earrings from the tip of one ear right down to the lobe.

'I wish!' says Nadine, who has been fighting a battle with her mum about body piercing for months and months.

We're running out of time. I'm not going to get picked.

I hold my picture up desperately – but he's looking the other side of the classroom, about to pick someone else.

'Pick Ellie!' says Magda.

'Yes, you must see Ellie's portrait,' says Nadine.

'Which one's Ellie?' says Mr Windsor.

'Me,' I mumble.

He looks at me and then he looks at my portrait. He looks at it a long long time while I wait, heart thudding.

'It's great,' he says. 'You really took in what I was saying last time, didn't you? This is fantastic.'

'What are you going to do to it, Mr Windsor?' asks Magda.

'I'm not going to do anything at all,' he says. 'It's perfect the way it is. It's such a powerful portrait. You're a true artist, Ellie.'

His words echo in my ears like heavenly bells. Then the real bell clangs and everyone grabs their stuff.

'Can I have a quick word, Ellie?' says Mr Windsor.

Magda and Nadine raise their eyebrows and nudge each other.

'Teacher's pet!' Nadine whispers.

'He could pet me all he wants,' Magda giggles.

'Behave yourselves, you two,' I say.

I go up to Mr Windsor while they clatter off.

'Can I hang on to your portrait, Ellie? I'd like to put it up on the wall if it's OK with you?'

'Sure.'

'Did you do the mural?'

'Some of it. With Zoë.'

'Which one was Zoë? Maybe you'd both like to come and do some extra Art at lunchtime?'

'She's not in my class. She's older. Only . . . she's in hospital.'

'Ah! Is she the girl with anorexia? They were talking about her in the staff room.'

'Yes.'

'What a shame. It sounds as if she had so much going for her too. I can't understand what makes girls starve themselves like that.'

'I don't think girls themselves understand either,' I say softly.

'Oh, well. Let's hope she gets better,' says Mr Windsor.

I nod, hoping and wishing and praying that poor Zoë really will get well.

'But anyway, you must feel free to come to the Art room any time, Ellie. With your two friends, if they want. Have you ever used oil paints? I think you'd love them. We'll give it a go sometime, right?'

'Right!' I say.

And with one bound the new powerful artistic talented me soars out of the classroom and down the corridor to join Magda and Nadine for lunch.